COPYRIGHT PAGE

AESON: BLACK
(The Atlantis Grail Novella Series)
Vera Nazarian

Cover Design by Vera Nazarian
"Bright, Blue Stars," Star cluster NGC 602 in the Small Magellanic Cloud, image credit NASA, January 14, 2021.

Trade Hardcover Edition
April 19, 2022

ISBN-13: 978-1-60762-179-9
ISBN-10: 1-60762-179-7

FIRST EDITION

A Publication of
Norilana Books
P. O. Box 209
Highgate Center, VT 05459-0209
https://www.norilana.com/
United States of America

AESON: BLACK

THE ATLANTIS GRAIL NOVELLA SERIES

VERA NAZARIAN

DEDICATION

For Elizabeth Logotheti,
Shoelace Girl and Astra Daimon

AESON: BLACK

I remove the black armband, dutifully fold it into a perfect square of silken fabric, and place it on the night stand near my bed.

The "night stand" varies, depending on where I sleep that night—in a crowded Fleet barracks, in the grand and solitary Crown Prince's Quarters at the Imperial Palace where every piece of ancient décor belongs in a museum, at my spacious home in Phoinios Heights filled with modern luxury, in a cramped crewman's shipboard cabin, or in somewhat more accommodating Fleet officers' quarters—such as *now*. Sometimes, the night stand is an antique piece of furniture made of priceless lacquered wood. At other times, it's a metal shelf emerging from a ship's hull, or a makeshift stack of items rising from the floor.

The ritual grounds me.

Ever since I awoke from the *black*, and drew my first, newly living breath, filled with an undefined but real *urge* and purpose, small rituals became important.

Such as tonight, here and now....

"Now" is a grim moment, six years later, on board the Imperial Command Ship 2—a Fleet vessel under my command, presently fulfilling the final stages of a complicated and fateful mission to Earth and back.

Early in the morning of this same day (three days before our scheduled arrival on Atlantis), I've had a soul-shattering conversation via interstellar with my Imperial Father. As soon as it ended, I disconnected our secure video call quantum comm link across the universe.

Then I called in my three Aides, all waiting outside my office—Gennio Rukkat, Anu Vei, and Gwen Lark. I told them that we've been ordered by My Father, the Imperator, to the Imperial Palace, as soon as we arrive in orbit, and that he expects to see Gwen Lark immediately, to be brought before him at Court that same evening. They must've noticed some of my initial agitation, especially in those first moments when I conveyed to them the Imperial orders—which is unforgivable of me.

What I did not tell them was the true gravity of this Imperial command and what it really means.

I'll never forget that call....

OUR EXCHANGE WAS PRECISE, unemotional, coldly controlled—a typical interaction between the Imperator and his Heir. And yet, something was different. A new sense of inner conviction arose inside me even as I listened to my Father's casual and terrifying words in regard to a *person* who has increasingly taken on significance for me.

This person, she—

I fixate on the Imperial words now, dwell on their cruel meaning, reliving our conversation. . . .

"As soon as you land, you'll bring the girl directly here," Romhutat Kassiopei, my Father and the Archaeon Imperator of *Atlantida* tells me during our call. "In fact, let's have her present at the Court Assembly as we welcome you home, so that I can have a first look at her while she's still—*fresh*. Afterwards, she'll be escorted straight to the research facility, and surrendered to the STA lab techs."

"Surrendered? For how long?" I ask in a neutral tone.

"As a potentially valuable asset she'll be held indefinitely. That *voice*. We must know how and why she has it; we must know *everything*. Fortunately, her Earth refugee status puts her in undefined territory—undefined, as in questionable rights— which gives us much . . . leeway. There might be legal concerns raised at some point, but not if we keep the whole operation quiet. This is now a matter of national security, not public scrutiny."

"I see." My tone remains steady and controlled, as I put every effort into keeping it blank, emotionless, same as the muscles of my face. . . .

"Will this be a problem for you?" The Imperial dragon rests the full force of his perceptive gaze on me.

"As long as basic ethical standards are upheld, none whatsoever," I respond at once, like an automated line of program code in a pre-ordained subroutine. I speak before I fully understand what is being said to me, before I allow myself to *feel*—knowing in advance that I must always employ the same perfectly bland, guarded subroutine with my Father when it comes to anything pertaining to *her*.

Allowing a precisely timed, casual pause, I ask, "What will happen to her?"

The Imperator observes me. After a close scrutiny for my gut reaction—and seeing none—he appears satisfied and continues, "She will become the property of the institute and undergo thorough study, a barrage of tests—full genome, neural activity, reproductive viability, and so on—under multiple stages of clearance. Starting with the first-level STA clearance. On Level One."

Basement Level One, or the Red Sector of the classified research facility underneath the *Stadion*, is a place I've come to know as a black site biological dissection lab, where certain human subjects disappear, never to see the light of day again. Subjects are invariably criminal convicts stripped of rights. Even so, the ethics of it always bothers me—has bothered me since the first time I visited the secret facility more than three years ago, on a cursory tour given by Shirahtet, the First Priest of Kassiopei.

"Do not be concerned, My Imperial Lord, they are murderous villains," Shirahtet informed me that day, speaking firmly, and I tried to take him at his word.

But not this girl, I think now, recalling that disturbing tour—small cells with listless or catatonic subjects held in restraints, prodded and questioned for hours by impassive techs, rooms of others attached to machinery and receiving chemical fluids, in some cases being vivisected. . . .

No!

Far from being a criminal, she is just a harmless young woman who works for me at the Central Command Office alongside my two regular Aides, Anu Vei and Gennio Rukkat. She's done nothing wrong except impossibly having the Logos voice of my Dynasty, a voice that she, a native of modern Earth, is not supposed to have—*she is innocent.*

Not only that, she is *extraordinary.*

Bright, talented, deserving the best opportunities and full personal freedom to live her life. And now she is being stripped of all rights, and will be treated as a specimen, experimented upon, inevitably *hurt*. . . .

An explosive surge of emotion strikes me. Fury and fierce rebellion soaked in despair overwhelm all reason. Suddenly there's a violent *need* to protect, to *rush* to her *now*, to stop the injustice, to do something, anything, to—do what? *What?*

I grow very still, halt my breathing . . . even as I battle to put down the ridiculous emotional storm with a cold force of will, restoring icy control of my veneer.

But the struggle continues. My traitorous mind presents me with endless images and details of *her*—who and what she is— young, intelligent, wildly creative and outspoken, a female Earth refugee whom I singled out for her potential and with whom I've interacted closely for the greater part of a year during our journey back to Atlantis.

Our interactions were . . . *still are* . . . complicated.

Furthermore, she is . . .

Gwen Lark.

She is—

Rawah bashtooh!

"Very well," my Father says after a small pause (and I have no way of knowing if he sees through me, recognizes my inner turmoil). "Make sure you have her ready and present at the Assembly. No need to inform her of the details, she will be processed afterwards. This way it will be easier for her . . . and for you."

"Consider it done," I respond, ignoring his last phrase. "Anything else?"

"No, this is sufficient for the moment. You may return to your duties. You have the last stages of Quantum Stream

Deceleration to worry about, and the logistics of processing millions of refugees," the Imperator says with an edge of sarcasm, still unraveling me with his gaze. "So, I'll leave you to it. Safe arrival!"

I respond with polite courtly words, and our call is concluded.

My secret inner response shocks me, and is still reverberating through me in a grim echo, like the effects of a Logos voice command. But I allow none of it to show, not even now, many hours later—even though I'm completely alone in my personal officers' quarters, with no witnesses to my reaction.

Of course, *completely alone* is only an assumption.

My Father has spies and surveillance equipment everywhere. Even light years away from my home planet and the Imperial Palace I cannot discount the likely presence of nano-cams, auto-dispatched to observe me alone in my cabin, to record my every breath and movement.

Indeed, my Father knows and suspects that Gwen Lark is important not only because of her voice, but because of what she *is* to me.

And what exactly *is* she to me?

Whatever it is, I must face it at last.

Here, now.

There's no more reprieve for me. . . .

To GROUND MYSELF, I return my attention to my neatly folded black armband that's presently lying on the narrow metal shelf jutting from the cabin hull. It's right next to the chair on which I sit and the modest cot on which I'll be sleeping tonight . . . eventually.

Such a claustrophobic, small space, my officers' quarters. Not much larger than other ship cabins, with a narrow cot, small desk and chair, wall-retractable, height-adjustable bathroom facilities and a shower stall. Yet it's sufficient for my needs. . . . (Distracted by these useless peripheral details, my mind attempts to wander, unwilling to face what must happen next, so I forcefully slam it back under control.)

I keep my mouth in a straight, controlled line as I focus on *nothing* but the square of black silk fabric and *think*.

One thing is certain. The ramifications of the conversation with my Father and my forthcoming decision are about to change the course of my life.

Right now, in this moment, I freely acknowledge what I've already *done* in my thoughts—or am about to do.

Done . . . will do . . . am doing. . . .

Yes, time occasionally *superimposes on itself* and blurs for me, ever since emerging from the *black*. It's been happening with diminishing frequency (as the event of my death recedes), but when it does, it's enough to briefly dissociate me from the present moment. Losing track of *then* and *now*, my mind swaps the chronology of events . . . a side effect of shared alien consciousness . . . for them, the *pegasei*, all time exists simultaneously or does not exist at all.

I turn back to my immediate present.

In this dire moment, even my heartbeat slows as the terror and thrill of my pending decision (with all its repercussions) combats within me. Light and dark, clarity and confusion.

The bonds of duty . . . or the freedom of . . . strange, unexplored emotions.

I am plunged in thought.

Plunged in *feeling*.

Once more it rises. . . . *Rawah bashtooh!* It rages inside me, swirling uncontrollably, like the forces of the accretion disk of Ae-Leiterra, which I somehow escaped—miraculously, unbelievably.

But—no. I did not escape so much as I was engulfed at the quantum level, given a dimensional *membrane* in order to halt my dissolution, and made to exist, disembodied, in some other separate *place*, without pain or worry or need or desire.

YES, time is blurring again, as soon as I think of it, allow myself the stupid, comforting distraction....

COMFORTING, because I was gently cocooned by alien frequencies spiraling all around me in a double helix, by strings of light . . . held together in a fixed vibration . . . held in place while I *resonated* dissonantly, teetered on the edge of dissolution (*varqood* Ae-Leiterra!), then settled into a stable phase . . . and ultimately was forced back into cohesive form (even as my physical outer shell was being ravaged—but no, it too was somehow partially *preserved* . . . just enough charred remains to give the human med techs something to work with as they restored my damaged body).

In short—I was forced back from chaos into an *information construct*—an entity, a sentience.

My own unique self.

Words are useless as I try to re-create the process of what was done to me by the shining alien beings whom we know as *pegasei*, a little over six years ago when I died on that fateful Rim Mission in the year 9764, a thirteen-year-old Imperial Prince fulfilling his duty to his bloodline.

To be honest, I don't understand or remember much of what happened when I died. Plunged into *black*, into nothing, and then a resumption.

And yet, what or where was I *in the interim* when I was dead?

What am *I*? What is death? What is the *black*?

Death is just another *membrane*.

According to the *pegasei*, it's a separator, not a thing unto itself. And it's so hard to put it into temporal words for the very reason that it is *not* temporal; it exists outside of space-time.

Death is a trans-dimensional quantum phase change that affects sentience.

Human physical science refers to death as *loss of information* —information is what makes any given entity what it is. And without the cohesiveness of an information construct, without a stable frequency resonance, there is no being, no life.

No meaningful pattern, no *order*.

If my Father only knew about these "exotic" thoughts I have, he would think me unfit to rule as his Heir.

Good thing he knows nothing about the pegasei *or what actually transpired.*

As always, once the retrospection begins, I cannot stop. I analyze the *black*, the oblivion. I've been given the rare opportunity to *understand* and self-reflect upon my own death, my own loss of timeline.

Therefore, I persist in trying to remember it . . . all of it.

Sometimes there are faint glimpses, and strange details emerge. In those details, I am *alien*. The rainbow quantum phase "cocoon" of the *pegasei* engulfs me and I distinctly feel the rushing stream of plural times, the universal river of data all *around* me that is full of *others* yet is also *me*.

Details of my life *before* death rush past me. . . . my earliest youth and childhood. They coalesce so far back that they come to the moment of my first conscious memory and my birth as an infant. However, like the flow of a great river, they *keep going*. . . .

Almost casually I recognize that the moment of my first "official" birth is also a resurrection from some *otherplace*, and that before it there were other details, other data, other lives.

There is life before birth. . . .

No, stop! Do not retreat that far back, it is not advisable. Instead, relive this life.

AND SO, details of my current existence engulf me.

One such detail (impossible, misunderstood, unrecognized by me for a long time) is the image of someone's *blue* eyes. I recall thinking of Elikara right before oblivion, and yet, the dissonance of that one detail—blue eyes instead of brown—confounds me.

Or at least it did, until *something* fell into place.

It happened some time after I met Gwen Lark.

I FLASH BACK to the year 9770—or Earth year 2047, according to their common modern calendar. The Fleet is stationed in low

Earth orbit—has been for months now, intentionally, so that our ark-ships are visible from the surface—and we've made our presence known to the global population.

In the course of overseeing aspects of the Qualification process, I am asked by my sole commanding officer on the Earth Mission, Imperial Fleet Commander Manakteon Resoi, to make random appearances at various Regional Qualification Centers, before choosing one RQC as my base of operation.

While I'm second-in-command of the Mission, I am also the Imperial Heir of *Atlantida*. We decide that for security purposes it would be best for me not to select an obvious high-profile urban center location such as New York, Beijing, Los Angeles, New Delhi, Moscow, London, but one of secondary importance. It would make me appear less conspicuous, and at the same time would permit me to observe and conduct my business. Meanwhile, the Commander himself and the other two Command Pilots of the Fleet will establish their presence at the more high-profile sites.

And so, I tour RQCs around the globe, settling on the major power players—China, United Industan, and the United States —but looking at the less prominent cities and regions within those nations.

On the first day of Qualification—while the children of Earth take their Preliminary Qualification aptitude tests (and the Fleet ark-ships ascend from lower orbit to a more secure one, no longer visible to the naked eye from the surface because it no longer matters to our purpose)—my two Aides and Command Deck officers run population demographics analysis programs and present me with a shortlist of the twenty most ideal, innocuous locations, and I begin to visit the ones that appear the most promising. In just a few hours I narrow down my preferences to five sites—two Chinese villages, a mid-sized settlement in United Industan on the shore of a large river, and two sites in the United States on the opposite coasts.

I dispatch various Pilots including *astra daimon* from my own Command Ship to the surface and assign them as official ACA-sanctioned Instructors on a trial basis to teach the first classes at these five sites that piqued my interest. Xelio Vekahat goes to a village in southern China, Erita Qwas to the river settlement in United Industan. Tiliar Vahad gets a small Oregon town on the West Coast of the United States, while Oalla Keigeri and Keruvat Ruo pair up to cover an East Coast location in Pennsylvania. As the ACA Imperial Liaison, Nefir Mekei tells me he will handle Culture instruction not only at the remaining central China village but at all five sites and report back with his personal recommendation.

By the second day of Qualification—the first official full day when the Pre-Qualified Candidates wake up in the morning in their new Dorms (having arrived the night before) and the actual classes begin—I take a shuttle down to the planet surface and make a quick series of stops on two Earth continents.

I observe the RQC compounds, the crop of Candidates at each, the surrounding environment. I attend the specific classes taught by my officer friends to get their final recommendations. By the end of the day, I'm leaning toward Vahad's picturesque and well-planned compound location in Willamette National Forest near Eugene, Oregon.

However, one more site remains, in Pennsylvania, where the last class of the day, Combat, is being taught by Keigeri and Ruo, which I expect to be a real showcase of both their stellar skills and antics, and an amusing look at their Earth students.

Indeed, Ker and Oalla do not disappoint. I land in Pennsylvania, walk from the airfield to the specific Dorm—all the while evaluating and examining this compound and finding it sufficient but less effective for my operational needs than the Oregon site—and follow the *daimon* to the designated basement floor gym.

There I see a terrified class of Candidates lined up in two rows opposite each other in the gymnasium hall. Compared to the trim and fit, highly focused teenagers I observed in China, or even their United States counterparts in Oregon, these young people are mostly in rough physical shape, with sloppy posture and poor control of their own bodies. Instead of being focused they appear resigned. Looking at this pathetic group I highly doubt that many of them will train well enough to Qualify.

Oalla introduces me in her playful hyperbole fashion as an "important visitor," almost defeating the purpose of my intended anonymity, and embarrassing me somewhat by her excessive praise. I'm presented as "Command Pilot Aeson Kass" —*Kass* being the name I've decided to use on Earth to draw attention away from my Imperial rank—and *"astra daimon"* is mentioned (to further aggravate me). Then she and Keruvat begin the Combat demonstration, starting with Quadrant weapons.

I stand aside and watch them and the class in action.

First, there are the usual warm-up exercises, during which the Candidates show themselves to be even more out of shape than I suspected. Much groaning and breathless panting and poorly executed movements. What do they even teach these Earth kids? Their education curriculum is obviously to blame, but with this particular group it could just be the luck of the draw, or even regional variation. . . .

As my thoughts coldly analyze the potential of this underwhelming lineup, Keruvat directs a Candidate to help him carry the weapons bag from storage to the floor for the Quadrant weapons demo. I watch the rest of the Candidates stagger upright from their apparently uncustomary physical exertions. Stilled in pitiful postures they wait for whatever comes next.

Ker empties the weapons bag, dumping its contents to the floor—nets and cords. I recall that this is a Yellow Quadrant Dorm. Oalla must really be enjoying herself. . . .

The two *daimon* begin the standard introductory weapons routine to demonstrate the Quadrant Circle of Dominance, sufficiently impressing everyone present with their speed and skills. I note stunned expressions among the Candidates, genuine amazement, dropped jaws, absolute *rapt attention*. Indeed, the simple elegance of how each Quadrant Weapon defeats the other and is dominated in turn, never fails to astound the first-time audience—on Earth or Atlantis.

(Here, childhood memories of my own first Combat demo come to me. I'm at the Imperial Palace sparring gym, my personal tutors preparing me early—long before Fleet Cadet School—as is suitable for the Imperial Heir).

When it's over, everyone claps, and I clap also—in their Earth manner of only putting palms together (as opposed to the Atlantean Fleet formal mode of striking the top of a closed fist with the palm of the other hand, or even the boisterous civilian manner of hitting one's own body parts and random nearest objects and even people).

Oalla rubs her arms where the *viatoios* armored sleeves protected her from the volley of projectiles that Ker just shot her way. "You have just learned the basic tenet of Atlantis weapons combat," she tells the class. "Yellow *cord* trumps Green *shield* trumps Blue *firearm* trumps Red *blade*, which in turn trumps Yellow *cord*. It's an eternal circular balance—a

Great Square. Somewhat like your Earth game of *paper-scissors-rock*."

I recall that the actual name of the Earth game is *rock-paper-scissors*, but don't bother to correct Instructor Keigeri before the class, since it would be inappropriate, not to mention trivial. Instead, I listen as Oalla and Keruvat handle the inevitable questions that follow.

A frightened girl wonders how they can learn all these weapons in so little time, which gives Keruvat the segue to discuss weaponless combat and introduce them to Er-Du.

Moments later, Oalla turns to me and once again puts me on the spot (even though, in no way do I show it—here, it's only my public face, blank and controlled). The girl is up to her usual antics.

"With your permission, Command Pilot Kass, may I have the honor, *daimon?*" Oalla asks me, motioning with her hand—an invitation to spar.

I pause, thinking, "*bashtooh*, Oalla," then nod.

These young Gebi are in for a shock.

And we proceed to fight before a room full of dumbstruck Earth boys and girls. I know this is instructional, and we have to show off a little to sell Er-Du, but I do feel bad for them, watching the two of us move and react with such preternatural speed. . . . No need to mention that Earth's lighter gravity makes our sparring workout that much easier for us.

That's the big secret. It probably makes us appear as superhuman and maybe even a little bit magical, but that's all it is—easy *gravity* combined with well-honed skills and reaction times. We've lived and trained under artificial Earth gravity for some time now, up on the ark-ships, during the journey here.

I'm not wrong about the impression we make. When Oalla and I are done, ending our demo with the Floating Swan, our breathing almost undisturbed, the Candidates appear stunned. They've been watching us do stuff they might see in the "movies" or "television"—the Earth version of media entertainment feeds.

I admit, I enjoyed myself. And yes, I'm amused, but keeping it in check. *Bashtooh*, Oalla.

Oalla steps back and lowers her head in the formal bow. "My profound thanks, *astra daimon*."

I nod to her, and straighten also, stepping out of the form. "A pleasure as always, *daimon* Oalla."

That's when a boy asks, "Wait, what? She's a *daimon* too? What's a *daimon* again?"

I mentally groan, watching how Ker and Oalla will extricate themselves from this delicate line of questioning. Ker begins explaining, mentions the Star Pilot Corps.

Oalla meanwhile glances back and forth at us. I can only hope that she realizes from my expression the need to be discreet and curtail this unnecessary topic.

Instead, it gets worse.

Oalla launches on a fierce explanation. "The *astra daimon* answer to no one but their own. We are a brotherhood and sisterhood, the best of the best," she tells the boy in her most imposing tone. "To be chosen as one of our brethren, a Pilot must earn the honor. The *astra daimon* have mastered the disciplines of at least one of the Four Quadrants. See this band on my arm?" She points to the yellow armband on her sleeve, then gives the boy a paraphrased version of the *astra daimon* secret creed.

"These are not mere 'dorm colors' as you might have seen on some of the other Instructors," Oalla says. "It is a symbol of my chosen discipline and Allegiance to the Yellow Quadrant."

Rawah bashtooh, Oalla, I'm tempted to interrupt, *enough*—

even as in my mind the familiar creed echoes; the sacred words of the oath to the brotherhood and sisterhood . . . words that I had to utter so many years ago, in another universe, so far away:

(*. . . I wear this band on my arm with honor. It is a symbol of my chosen discipline and Allegiance to the Blue Quadrant. . . .*)

"As mine is to the Blue Quadrant," Keruvat says just then, narrowly echoing my thoughts and pointing to his own blue armband sleeve.

Varqood it, not you too, Ker. . . .

"And what about him?" the same boy asks again, and points directly at *me*. "Is he some kind of black ninja?"

Some of the Candidates respond with stifled laughter, a nervous reaction which we ignore. But now everyone is focused on my black armband.

Great. . . . I can just imagine the unnecessary explanations that will be forthcoming *now* from my two so-called friends. . . .

I watch the questioner, a tall, dark-skinned youth with long, tightly woven locks of hair. Directly next to him, a girl with slouching posture shifts from one foot to the other in discomfort and turns to look at him, most likely in an attempt to make him stop talking.

Just for a moment I feel a ridiculous sense of affinity with her, since both of us appear to be *aware*, in our own way, of the wrongness of this turn of conversation.

Probably for quite different reasons, I think with a pang of amusement. This girl—and the rest of them—are terrified. Me? I'm merely annoyed at my dearest friends and their big, flapping mouths.

Oalla hones in on the boy who asked the unfortunate question. "Your name, Candidate?"

He mumbles some nonsense then says his name is "Tremaine Walters."

"Tremaine Walters, you think this is funny?" Oalla glares at him.

And then she and Ker both outdo themselves, just as I feared.

"The black color of his armband means that this *astra daimon* has *died* on our behalf," Oalla reprimands. "He has given his life once for the Fleet and his brethren, and he was brought back, and we are forever indebted to him—all of us, indeed, all of Atlantis."

"A black armband is the highest honor, and is usually earned posthumously—after death. Command Pilot Aeson Kass is a rare exception. He is one of the few in our history who has the right to wear the black armband while living." That part comes from Ker, who should know better.

The class was stunned before, but now they've stopped breathing.

"All right, any more questions, before we proceed?" Oalla asks loudly.

Silence.

And then, a girl's clear voice sounds. "Yes, I have a question..."

It's the same girl, the one who's been fidgeting next to the tall, dark boy. She raises her hand unnecessarily, after she's already begun to speak. "Why? Why all this? Why must there even *be* Combat? Why do we need to learn to fight, and hurt, and possibly kill other people, in order to Qualify for just being alive? Doesn't Atlantis have some kind of organized legal system so that the average citizen doesn't need to engage in violence? I mean—"

As she babbles, her voice gains energy, resonance, and confidence, words tumbling faster and louder. Then it fizzles out into awkward silence. And yet, the curious *sentience* of her question is undeniable.

The gym hall is perfectly quiet. Ker and Oalla appear to be briefly stumped by this unexpected, inquisitive outburst.

I examine the girl. She is skinny and tall, not bad looking, but nothing out of the ordinary—an oval face and light skin, flushed from the exertion of exercise, surrounded by sweaty tangles of unruly brown hair. A few tendrils are stuck to her forehead. . . . Again, that poor posture and slouching shoulders, as though she's trying to disappear into herself like a turtle.

But then she turns her face somewhat and I catch her expression directly.

Her eyes. . . .

Their sharp blue *clarity* connects with me. And before I even think to second-guess my action, I find myself answering her.

"You ask why we are required to fight?" I speak, focused on her eyes. "In Atlantis, we believe in taking responsibility for ourselves. As you learn to fight, you learn to defend yourself from physical harm. You acquire a powerful self-preserving skill set, and a specific attitude. This attitude carries across to other aspects of your life. So that you can defend yourself from other *less tangible* but far more dangerous things that can break you—not just your body, but your spirit. Things such as deception, corruption, disparagement, coercion, false accusation and persecution. Subtle evil things that undermine *you*. And if you can maintain the inner ability to defend yourself against influence, you can build a *purpose* in your life that no one can take away from you."

I pause, surprised at my own eloquence, continuing to look at her, even as she holds my gaze with her *clear* eyes and appears unflinching (or maybe she's petrified with fear—either guess is good right now). Then I continue because there's more to say, and it needs to be said, "In Atlantis, we believe that purpose is the most important virtue. You can lose your freedom, your health, your honor, everything you love and care about. And yet, if you still have your purpose, you have lost nothing."

My words are cutting and precise, while my voice unintentionally rises to near-Logos level, as I conclude, "Does that answer your question?"

She nods silently. And does not break off her gaze.

Which means that *I* must.

I turn away—or rather tear myself away—from the strange contact, and force myself to return my attention to Keruvat and Oalla.

I indicate to them to continue the class.

Thankfully, Oalla gets back to work, shouting at the two rows of young Gebi.

"Candidates! You will now learn the basic Forms of Er-Du! Watch and follow me!"

As I make the effort to observe the room, I feel a burning sense of being examined from the back, as if that *girl* is somehow still fixated on me. . . .

Ridiculous sensation. I attempt to shake it off, even as I become aware, peripherally, of a tangible easing of tension all around the room, followed by a resumption of exercise. . . .

But my focus is ruined, my attention oddly diluted. I struggle to properly observe the class as Ker and Oalla demonstrate the Forms.

Eventually the otherwise pathetic class ends, and the rest of the day is unremarkable. However, I am faced with making a decision as to which RQC to choose for my base of operations.

I consult with Keruvat and Oalla, call Tiliar, Erita, and

Xelio who are all still at other locations, and Nefir, who is up on ICS-2 doing his official reporting to the ACA and my Father.

And then I somehow convince myself in a roundabout way that—despite the fact that Tiliar's Oregon RQC site is a far better choice overall—there is something about this Pennsylvania compound that feels like it should be my official site. . . .

Something.

Not sure what manner of *shar-ta-haak* reasoning leads me to this serious decision, what flimsy logic, but I decide to work from *here*. That evening I inform Commander Resoi and make it official.

The next day my office is formally established and all necessary secure tech hardware is brought down to the planet surface. All personnel under my command are recalled to Pennsylvania RQC-3 to be formally stationed at the compound, and our work begins.

At the end of that same day—after eating the late afternoon meal that Earth people call dinner, just as we head back to our row of offices on the upper floors of the large Arena Commons complex, moving along the narrow balcony walkway—I happen to look down on the ground floor where hundreds of Candidates are eating in the courtyard.

And I see the girl from the day before—the one who asked the intelligent question and somehow disturbed me. In that moment of strange coincidence, she looks up exactly in my direction—again, as if she *knows* I see her. Our gazes meet. A brief contact, followed by recognition, I'm certain, but enough. . . .

I see the clarity of her look. My gaze is halted, fixed on hers, across the expanse of the arena, down several floors. It is a line of energy cast through wide space between us, a projectile fired and anchored.

I look away at once and keep walking, listening to Xel and Erita's laughing banter, Nefir's voice as he argues jokingly with Keruvat, Oalla's teasing tone.

That girl with her clear-eyed gaze remains below.

I briefly wonder what her name is.

Gwen Lark.

I will not find out her name for quite some time—not until days later.

RESURFACING from that first memory of meeting *her*, I continue to stare at the folded piece of black silk. The onslaught of thoughts mingled with memories floods me, until I'm drowning in conflicting urges.

I must sink back, go even deeper into the ocean of my mind to corroborate my life-changing decision. No time to waste; the end of the journey is almost here. Arrival on Atlantis looms before me.

My black armband. . . . Ah, at what cost.

WHEN I WOKE up from my death all those years ago, I was changed. A layer of innocence stripped away, youthful naïveté transformed to a deeper sense of *knowledge*. And yet, this added secret layer of *something new and serene* in the depths of my mind was not immediately available to my conscious mind.

My memories are muddled even now.

I recall those early days of being back in a healed, new version of my body, the army of medical techs running every imaginable test on me, my Father and Mother fussing over me to such an extent that I've never seen before—my Imperial Father, especially.

He checked up on me constantly, came into my room and made actual physical contact—*touched* me, felt my forehead and jaw, told me to widen my eyes and open my mouth, breathe into various apparatus—and called for medics in a hard voice whenever he thought something was wrong with my numbers.

It is such a rare thing, to have my Father be so concerned. If I hadn't been so *numb* in those early days, I might have responded more, *enjoyed* it, but as such, it is all dreamlike, half-real. . . .

Until I remember how it happened, how he stayed back in the shuttle at the Rim of Ae-Leiterra and allowed me to sacrifice myself in his stead. And my *numbness* closes in and solidifies.

My poor *Mamai*, she knows something is off about me. I'm too calm, too distant and emotionally reserved, even with her—and oh, how it worries her. . . .

They and everyone else ask me repeatedly what I remember—the same wrong questions—and I tell them I remember nothing about being dead.

It is neither accurate, nor true, but it is all I'm capable of telling. How am I to explain that *memory itself* is precisely what death cuts off?

Then the next hazy days and weeks follow, as I recover more of my former personality. Physically, my body is in top shape due to medical regeneration tech. I am slightly weak in the first few days as my new muscles learn their tone, but I gain strength quickly.

It is my mind that's *strange*, for lack of a better word. The Palace staff keep a close eye on me under the strict instructions of my Father, and I'm not even permitted to watch the media feeds or entertain visitors.

Slowly I begin to participate in my ordinary life. My friends are finally allowed to see me, ready to embrace me (although, much initial awkwardness takes place). Next, I am permitted to leave the confines of my Palace Quarters, and even report to the Fleet HQ for light duty (my Father insists I don't "overexert myself").

It must be said that at this point, Oalla, Erita, Keruvat, Xelio, Tiliar, and the others are all in the Star Pilot Corps, and are high-ranking pilots. Some of them have become *astra daimon*. All this time they've been advancing their careers and flying to the stars, while I've been moping and stewing in my own self-made pit of depression and punishment.

Each of my friends can brag about being deployed on exciting missions to the various Hel system stations and outposts. I alone remain planet-bound with the Imperial Fleet, stubbornly denying myself what I once wanted above all else in life—a life in the SPC....

I continue to grieve the loss of Elikara—or at least it's what I tell myself, trying to justify my choice to remain in the IF as an underachieving Pilot, Third Rank.

But it is all inconsequential now. What's done is done.

I have evolved. The flooding river of *universal sentience* rushes through me—occupying that same hidden layer of my mind of which I'm now permanently aware. I may not access it consciously, but I know it's there—thanks to the *pegasei*. And it has awakened the old drive in me, the will and desire to *achieve*, and to make a difference in this world.

And so, on the first day of my return to the Fleet Headquarters I'm ready to announce my intentions to my commanding officer: I'll be applying for transfer to the Star Pilot Corps after all.

As I walk into the familiar, sprawling old building near the business center of Poseidon, I'm met with stares, whispers, and looks of *awe*.

Every officer, every cadet, every rank pilot in the hallways stops to look at me and, in many cases, to *thank me*. Officers of many ranks above my own straighten and halt before me, saluting me. Even the civilian building staff pause to give me bows. . . . Somehow, I doubt they are saluting the Imperial Heir, but something else—*someone* else.

What is going on?

Fortunately, near the doors of the IF Command Office, I run into Keruvat. Ker is wearing the everyday grey Fleet uniform with the addition of the SPC insignia patch. I'm reminded that he also has a tiny *astroctadra* pin attached to the underside of the blue armband on his sleeve. . . .

The pin is practically invisible and unobtrusive, and no one would know it's there unless they knew where to look. I've discovered it once by accident, seeing him fold his armband after our sparring practice, and asked about its meaning, but Ker gave me a strained look and said that it's nothing. Knowing Ruo's basic integrity and inability to obfuscate, I suspect that it has something to do with the *astra daimon*.

Keruvat is the first one of my friends to be invited into the exclusive *astra daimon* brotherhood and sisterhood, soon after his comet mining mission. During that mission he not only supervised a pilot team but did some amazing, high-precision solo flight maneuvers—some of which ended up being taught in Fleet Cadet School—and word gets around. As one of the *daimon*, he is only permitted to publicly admit what he is, but may not say anything about the details of the initiation (despite being nagged about it by Xelio, Oalla, and the others).

And now, Ker sees me in the hall and his eyes widen with warmth. "Kass!" he says. "They let you out already? *Bashtooh!* How do you feel?"

"Quite well, thanks," I respond. "I'm back, on my way to see the Command about an upgrade—to the SPC."

Ker makes an amazed and happy sound. "Seriously?"

"Yes."

"Hah! *Finally!* You've changed your mind! *Bashtooh*, we're going to mark the occasion tonight!" Ker slaps his palm against his abdomen and makes a celebratory fist. And then he adds, "You're up to it, right? It's all right if you're not. I know you've been locked up in the Palace for days, after the you-know-what...."

Keruvat still finds it awkward to mention my death, so he refers to it in roundabout fashion. Together with the others he's only been allowed to see me a couple of times at home in my Palace Quarters as I was forcibly recuperating, and the whole thing has been somewhat strained and weird.

As I recall, my friends didn't know what to say to me in the first moments when they entered my room and saw me seated (despite all my protests) in a medical chair like an invalid. Oalla promptly hugged me and started to cry; Erita just stood there and touched my arm with a kind of reverence; Xelio glared at me with glistening eyes, then cussed me out for "dying without permission." Only Keruvat paused at the door, holding back, with an unusual reserve—just a hint of distrust in his eyes—then took a deep breath and approached me. Yes, they all got over it, but Ker seemed to have the most trouble dealing, so it took him a bit longer—possibly something having to do with his family's religious beliefs and a small degree of superstition.

"I am completely ready for anything and everything," I reply now with a faint smile of amusement. It occurs to me that this is one of my first actual smiles since my "resurrection." The *numbness* has been slowly fading, and the normal human emotions are again surfacing. "But first," I say, "I need to go inside and take care of this."

"Sure, of course!" Ker says. "I was on my way out, but I'll wait for you. Go, get in there, Kass! SPC is calling you!"

"I have to ask," I say, lingering before the doors. "Do you know what—what exactly do they think of me? How much does everyone know? Just now, on my way here, I saw people staring, superior officers saluting. Why?"

Ker wrinkles his forehead. "Why? What do you mean, why? You don't know? You forgot? You saved the entire Fleet at Ae-Leiterra, man! You're a national hero!"

AFTER THAT STRANGE but obvious revelation—strange to me because, again, I've apparently existed in a halfway-dream state for the last week, unaware of real-world events which were kept from me by my overprotective parents—I find that not only does the whole Fleet think of me as a hero, but so does the entire country.

The network feeds are full of people discussing my actions, while the miracle that brought me back is somehow underplayed, or at least never particularly questioned. They must attribute it to our high-tech medicine, and no one even mentions the *pegasei's* presence and exact location at that moment along the Rim when I reinforced the Stationary Quantum Stream Boundary and Breached to my death.

They enveloped me with their rainbow light. . . . They kept me in a different quantum phase. . . . Or maybe when I was a part of the

*great stream I merely slipped away into the Afterlife, which in itself
is an ocean of mingled souls—*

As for what happens after I go inside the Imperial Fleet
Headquarters office for my meeting with Fleet Command?

I merely bring up my interest in Star Pilot Corps, and
immediately my upgrade request is accepted by the officer in
charge. He transmits my personnel file, accompanied by his
stellar recommendation, to the SPC Headquarters located on
the Atlantis Space Station orbiting the planet.

"Pilot Kassiopei, naturally, I grant your transfer. You will
begin your new assignment as soon as we hear back from the
Station Nomarch, Evandros," the officer tells me. "He must still
approve your new rank and placement personally, but it's a
formality. After what you've done—what you've accomplished
on behalf of the Fleet and all of Atlantis—your position at the
SPC is guaranteed."

And just like that, I am in the Star Pilot Corps.

I admit, it's almost irritating. I would've preferred to have to
work for it, to prove my suitability, to be challenged by the SPC
Command for a chance at acceptance. . . .

And then again, like a *hoohvak*, I remember . . . I died for it.

There is nothing more to prove.

The next day I fly a personal shuttle (my first solo orbital
flight since my return from the *black*) up to the SPC
Headquarters, and for the first time I meet the man who will
shape the rest of my military life.

Nomarch Ayan Evandros. Stern, fair, thorough, relentless.
His appearance is middle-aged, with bronze leathery skin, dark
hair greying at the temples and the bare minimum of gold dye.
He examines me and asks me clever placement questions
designed to elicit emotional responses from me—which I do

not give (having had the long practice of wearing my impassive public mask with my Imperial Father).

Evandros shows no emotion either, neither in his questioning nor his reactions to my responses, so during that first unforgettable meeting the two of us appear to spar on equal footing with deceptively calm words.

Finally, he must be satisfied by what I give him. "Congratulations, Pilot Kassiopei," he tells me. "I am assigning you to this Station. Green Amrevet 2, Blueday, will be your first day. Check in at seventh hour of Ra and report to me, promptly —regardless of any Landing Day Holiday festive excesses of the night before. Do not assume that, just because they give you the black armband, you're not subject to constant scrutiny for your performance."

For the first time I allow myself to express something. "They give me *what?*" I ask quietly, but my tone reveals my surprise.

Did I hear right?

Evandros looks at me closely, and for the first time a brow twitches with some kind of reaction of his own. "You don't know? You're being awarded the usually posthumous black armband of High Service to *Atlantida*."

"I—no, I didn't know," I reply. "When? How?"

A barely perceptible spark of energy comes to the older man's dark eyes. He must recognize my genuine confusion. And just for an instant he reveals amusement. "Ah . . . I regret spoiling your surprise. The ceremony is scheduled for a week and a half from today, but you will be hearing more about it from other sources—"

"You mean my Imperial Father?"

"Yes, and the Imperial Fleet High Command."

I shake my head in continued amazement, and find myself

looking away from the astute and perceptive gaze of the Station Nomarch.

He managed to stump me after all.

~

FROM THAT POINT ON, events happen quickly. If my memories serve me true, I assume my new basic duties of an entry-level SPC Pilot on the first work day of the year 9765.

And then a few days later, in a grand Ceremony at the *Kemetareon* in Poseidon, attended by everyone of consequence in both the Fleet and Court, I am awarded the black armband by my Imperial Father and the IF Commander Manakteon Resoi. The irony of that juxtaposition of events, on so many levels, never escapes me.

"For your High Service to this grateful Nation and to Me, I award you the ultimate Honor," the Imperator declares in his Logos voice that resonates with power throughout the wide expanse of the brightly illuminated forum packed with audience, then indicates with one finger for the two waiting officers to proceed.

They approach me with the black armband, as part of a wreath arrangement normally accorded to the dead.

Normally this wreath is presented to the bereaved family, the widow or widower. . . . The recipient's body wears the black armband at the funeral, and is cremated or buried with it. . . .

In my case, the IF Commander steps forward and unwinds the black silk from the wreath, while complete silence fills the great *Kemetareon*. . . .

Time both focuses and dilates for me. My gaze momentarily comes to rest on the face of my Mother, the Imperatris, seated on the throne next to my Father. I see her intense, glistening

eyes full of love . . . and next to her, my young sister Manala—
fragile and introspective—watches me with similar tear-filled
eyes.

"Pilot Aeson Kassiopei. From this moment forward, until
your final breath, you relegate your Quadrant allegiance to
second place. You will now wear the Honor of *Atlantida* on your
sleeve."

Commander Resoi speaks formally, removing the Blue
armband encircling my White dress uniform sleeve and
replacing it with the black piece of silk—even as my Father
watches from his throne a few steps away, watches me with the
stone gaze of a dragon. . . .

Afterwards, I stand immobile, my arm now wrapped in
black, while endless Imperial Fleet officers march past me, with
honor salutes. My new commanding officer, Nomarch Evandros
is among them, representing my new affiliation with the Star
Pilot Corps—even though this is not an SPC event. This is the
first time that Evandros salutes me, and the only time as my
superior officer. . . .

Indeed, who am I now? Whom do I truly serve?

The only thing different is that black piece of fabric around
my sleeve.

BACK IN THE PRESENT MOMENT, I continue to focus on my black
armband as selective memories swirl in my mind, aiding me
with my ultimate decision. Though, not sure how *this* particular
one serves me . . . it's the memory of another striking day that
comes months later, at the end of the same year 9765.

It's Blue Ghost Moon 26, New Year's Eve, the end of my first
year at the SPC. I choose to take part in a low-key evening

celebration with my friends, before having to endure the traditional formality of the Imperial Palace New Year's Day feast at my Father's table all of the following day, not to mention the even more strict Landing Day ceremonies and rituals on the day immediately after.

We're all back at Poseidon for this stretch of holidays. It's been a long year, but it flew by in a daze of established routine and highly focused, precision-filled tasks—piloting patrol missions in deep space, Fleet training maneuvers, military vessel systems analysis, inventory, star chart memorization, crew and officer interactions, achieving familiarity with every one of our space stations (down to the smallest Hel system planetary and moon orbital and surface outpost), and my first command assignments on smaller missions.

And now we're on leave, the majority of the SPC personnel back down on the surface of Atlantis, many of us scattered around the globe in our respective home countries.

My friends and fellow SPC Pilots who are Imperial *Atlantida* natives are staying around the capital city, at their homes or with family. My own Imperial Family insists I reside at the Prince's Quarters in the Palace during those days and not at my own personal estate in Phoinios Heights which I would normally prefer.

Our evening get-together is hosted by Oalla Keigeri, at the Keigeri Family town residence. Lord Desher Keigeri wisely makes himself absent that night to give us the freedom to be ourselves. The party starts at seventh hour of Khe, with a *niktos* meal, followed by the usual entertainment nonsense as we hang out together and see where the night takes us around town.

Keruvat is supposed to pick me up so that we arrive a few daydreams after seventh hour. Although I've only been back home for less than a full day, the familiar overbearing atmosphere of the Imperial Palace and all it entails already weighs down on me, so I'm eager to get out.

Using my best stealth skills, I slip past my Imperial guards and head downstairs to the Palace gardens near the airfield to meet him. I manage this feat by exiting through the small exterior door in my workroom normally used only by my Aides and Palace staff, then take my private elevator.

Savoring my escape, I emerge into the deepening twilight of the small garden courtyard. As I turn into the park, I see the familiar figure of Oalla. She's walking quickly along the gravel path toward me. The light orbs are just starting to bloom with artificial illumination, and they cast a warm glow on Keigeri's undeniably serious, possibly anxious face.

Something must be wrong.

"Is everything okay?" I ask with concern. "Where's Ker? What are you doing here, instead of being at your own party?"

Oalla stops and grabs me by the arm. "*Bashtooh*, Kass, didn't you check your messages? I just texted you I was coming to get you, told Ker to look after the party and let people in until I get back. We need to go somewhere else, right *now!*"

"Huh?" I pause, feeling my forehead tense up. "No, I didn't check my texts. What's going on?"

Oalla drops my arm and glares at me with an intense expression. "You've been *called out* by someone," she says grimly.

"What?" I pause, looking at her. "You don't mean—"

"Called out! For wrongdoing," she elaborates. "Yeah, it's exactly what you think it is, unfortunately."

I am stunned.

Being "called out" is an invitation to an honor fight.

"No, that's not possible. Who is it?" I ask softly in a cool, measured tone that I've cultivated to deal with stressful situations. "Who called me out? What kind of *shebet* is this—?"

"I don't know!" she exclaims, grabbing my arm again, this time with a painful grip. "Some *chazuf* stopped me in the Fleet HQ hallway this afternoon, when I was picking up some stuff. He must've known that I'm a friend of yours, and told me some guy was looking for you. Didn't tell me his name, just that he's a Pilot, Second Rank, and the guy randomly picked him to be his witness."

"That's impossible. I didn't wrong anyone—not that I can think of, at least not recently." I continue to speak coldly even as I stare at Oalla, no longer seeing her. Rehashing the events of the past few days, I try to recall if I've argued with anyone, or was rude. . . .

Oalla discerns my exact thoughts in her typical astute fashion. "Did you, maybe elbow some guy in the meal hall? Maybe, get in his way, cut in line ahead of him, or step on his foot by accident? Gambled and won against someone's passionate bet?"

"Huh? *What?* No!"

And then something else occurs to me. Oalla was randomly picked to deliver me the news, which means, *she* is now my official witness. A "witness" in this context is the reliable person on your side who accompanies you to the honor fight to assist with the details but otherwise acts as a bystander.

Varqood, *is that where we're going now? To an honor fight?*

I stand petrified like a fool, frowning hard, until Oalla tugs my arm for the third time. "Let's go! We have to go now—they're waiting for us."

"But—what about your party?" Admittedly, that's the stupidest thing I've said so far.

She shakes her head with annoyance, confirming my stupidity. "Ker's handling it, I told you."

"Does he know about this?"

"*Bashtooh*, no," she replies grimly. "I did *not* tell Ker. You know how he would react . . . I couldn't tell him. He'd come running to protect you. Or get rid of the guy's body after you killed him."

"I wouldn't kill—I would speak with this person, reason with him. There won't be any fighting—"

"I know. Let's just deal with it, Kass."

Generally speaking, honor fights are frowned upon, considered semi-legal, punishable by Fleet demerits and worse, and the fewer people are involved, the better. Only the injured parties and their witnesses are expected to be present, and that's it.

I draw a deep breath and regain my ability to move. "All right, let's get it over with. Where to?" I ask, as we start to walk rapidly through the park toward the airfield.

"Not sure, except the address is south of downtown. Could be near the Bay," she says. "Wherever it is, likely an abandoned building."

And she's right.

We take her hovercar, flying some distance over the bright winking dots of light that make up the night city, heading toward the ocean. Oalla is unusually quiet, letting me speak, and so gets to listen to me methodically reason out loud how all of this must be a *hoohvak* misunderstanding. I'm aware that I can be tedious sometimes, but right now my sense of outrage is simmering and must have a logical outlet.

We come down in an industrial area, and the location is indeed an old business structure, empty and dark. Dilapidated walls, cracks and broken windows and exposed metal supports. Oalla double-checks the address then cusses softly.

"I'm really not in the mood for a sparring workout," she grumbles, hover-parking her expensive vehicle in the best-lit section of the empty lot nearby, and we get out. "This better not be an ambush or scam. Too bad you ditched your guards; we could've used some backup, or at least personal insurance as to the safety of the Imperial Heir to the Throne."

"If it is, we'll deal with it," I say through my teeth. I'm suddenly very angry now—angry at this whole idiocy, angry that someone thought it was okay to waste my time like this, knowing I cannot refuse on pain of dishonoring a Fleet tradition. Add to this my distaste at being the trending topic on all the public gossip feeds.

Because I'm certain I've wronged no one.

And I don't do honor fights. Instead, what I do is *resolve conflicts*, as I've demonstrated repeatedly over the months of my being at the SPC.

We turn on portable orb lights, set them loose to hover-float ahead of us, and approach the dark building. After trying a couple of sealed entrances, Oalla finds a door that's been left unlocked.

She pulls it open and I follow her inside.

Our Fleet-issue light drones bounce around in the air, marking a well-defined perimeter around us and following a zig-zag reconnaissance pattern of programming. They cast multiple shadows against walls, revealing a vast warehouse space with abandoned shelving and scaffolding everywhere.

This is an ugly location.

Oalla stops to check her wrist unit, and keys in something. "Hold on," she says, lifting one hand to stop me. "Just need to respond to Ker, he's asking questions."

I raise one brow but say nothing as I pause, my posture deceptively relaxed, every muscle in my body ready to spring into action. Meanwhile my attention is fully on our surroundings.

My accuser is not here yet, or at least no one is visible. I don't expect whoever it is that called me out to be hiding from me.

And then, I see multiple movement.

Numerous shadows separate from the distant walls and rows of shelving structures all around the hall, moving toward us from all directions. . . . From overhead, near the distant ceiling, figures on hoverboards descend and spring down onto the floor with sleek, silent movements of highly-trained fighters. There are dozens of them. And more keep coming.

Definitely, an ambush.

The figures advance. Just then, as if on cue, our orb lights go out.

"*Shebet . . .*" I mutter through my teeth. My heart pounds with angry energy, and a frisson of alarm passes through my nerve endings—not quite fear, but emergency preparedness. To my discredit, I didn't anticipate an honor fight that involves going up against a large, hostile gang in pitch-black darkness.

As the future Imperator, I should've anticipated this and everything else—all possible outcomes, especially when it comes to enemy moves. . . .

Furthermore, I'm an irresponsible fool for not having my personal guards with me. This situation—it's what I deserve for trying to evade the clearly delineated confines of my duty.

(. . . avoid my destined duty, bypass my obligations . . . so that's why this memory surfaces now. . .)

. . .

I FEEL Oalla's sudden grip on my wrist. *Bashtooh* . . . the additional realization hits hard—*Oalla* is here with me. She shouldn't be involved in something like this. . . .

A stab of worry on Keigeri's behalf strikes me. Yes, Oalla can more than take care of herself, but there's only two of us, and we'll be fighting an army, blind. If something happens to her, Ker will kill me, not to mention, *I* will kill me. . . .

Just as I take my fighting stance, honing my hearing to compensate for the darkness, Oalla's entirely unexpected, ringing-loud voice sounds at my side.

"Aeson Kassiopei! You have been called out by one of your peers and you must answer!"

As soon as she speaks, the lights go on. That is, our own light drones reactivate, and several additional light orbs bloom into existence, like stars being born. They converge and float in a calm, circular formation all around us, revealing the hall and everyone in it.

I blink, seeing figures close in slowly from all directions, packing into all available space and forming a crowd. . . . Except —I *know* them.

Keruvat is here! I notice him first, since he towers over others near him. I start to wonder if Oalla called him for help, but then I see *other* friends.

Erita is standing in a loose stance; there's Tiliar, with his arms folded; Nefir, staring at me with a kind of transfixed expression; Xelio, straight-backed and grave. . . . Also, Radanthet, Nergal, Culuar, Quoni, Abaivara. . . . the list goes on.

Familiar Pilots and officers from the Star Pilot Corps surround us, in frightening, perfect silence. Some are casual acquaintances, some I've barely interacted with, and a few others are entirely unknown to me. Of the ones I recognize, it occurs to me that all of them have the reputation of excellence. These men and women are exemplary Fleet officers and top-skilled Pilots. For some reason they're all here, and they're all staring at us—at *me*.

What the hell is going on?

I cast a quick, confounded glance at Oalla, as she suddenly takes a few steps, backing away from me, and joins the greater circle around us—no, around *me*, since now I remain alone, surrounded.

"Oalla, what—" I begin.

"Aeson Kassiopei!" Oalla repeats loudly, facing me with a serious expression that I find the most disturbing of all in this bizarre moment.

And then my heart jumps at the thunderous noise, because the entire room echoes her. . . .

"Aeson Kassiopei!"

They all speak my name in unison.

"You have been called out by one of your peers and you must answer!" Keigeri says again.

"Who calls out this Pilot?" a male voice asks in a similar loud manner, somewhere from the back of the circle. And at once the phrase is repeated variously by everyone. "Who calls out this Pilot?"

"I call out this Pilot!" The speaker is Xelio Vekahat.

Xel steps out of the circle and approaches me, stopping to face me at arm's length. "And now he must answer."

"*Bashtooh*, Xel," I mutter. "What—"

"Pilot, you have been observed and you have been found—lacking," Xel interrupts in a formal tone, and his expression is so fiercely *controlled* that for a crazy instant I imagine he's holding back amusement. He continues, turning his head unexpectedly to address the circle of others around us, "What is this Pilot lacking?"

"Lacking dishonor!" Keruvat says.

"Lacking cowardice!" Erita says.

"Lacking—I don't know, *sha* brains?" Oalla says suddenly, and there is a wave of laughter.

Xel meanwhile turns his attention back to me. "Answer me truly—will you uphold honor or throw it away? Will you stand in strength as one of us or will you flail in the wind? Will you pledge yourself freely to the *astra daimon?*"

Only then it finally hits me.

I've been allowed entry into the secret brotherhood and sisterhood, and this is the initiation ceremony.

I can hardly believe it. . . . A very long-standing dream of mine is happening right now, coming true. And Xelio, of all people, is the one to bring me into the fold. . . .

I knew he was made *astra daimon* quite a while ago, not too long after his exemplary work at Ishtar Station (as have most of my friends in the SPC, showing their excellence during various field assignments), but for some reason I find this particular situation both touching and ironic.

I hesitate for only a moment, keeping my mouth in a tight, controlled line. And then I reply, "Yes . . . I will."

There is a suspenseful pause.

"Very well, Kass," Xel says in a suddenly casual tone, and his expression relaxes. He draws very close to me and rests his hand on my upper arm, directly over my black armband.

"Repeat after me," he continues—his face so near mine that the flickering reflection of many orb lights softens the overwhelming intensity of his black eyes—and then intones loudly: "I wear this band on my arm with honor. It is a symbol of my chosen discipline and Allegiance to the Blue Quadrant underneath the Black, to my *sen-i-senet*, and to my true self. By the Star, I pledge myself to the *astra daimon*."

I slowly repeat the words, feeling a wild, unspeakable energy race through me, raise the hairs along my skin with awe, and fill my heart. . . . This energy, it's the kind of fierce joy that I haven't felt since earliest childhood, and not at all since I died at Ae-Leiterra.

When I'm done, the hall erupts with applause, shouts, and inspired voices exclaiming, "By the Star! *Saret-i-xerera!*"

"*Wixameret*, heart brother, you are now *astra daimon*," Xelio says, grinning at me. "Congratulations, *chazuf*, you're one of us!"

"That's it?" I say, finding myself grinning also. "No bloodletting? No arcane rituals where I'm forced to eat some pickled *bakris?*"

"Yeah, that's it," Keruvat says coming up to me and slapping me on the back. "Unless you want me to get you some pickled *bakris?*"

"Well, you also get this little pin," Erita adds, coming up from my other side and offering something tiny and golden, sparkling in her palm. "By the Star!"

"No, don't just let him take it!" Oalla intervenes. Before I can reach for the pin, she grabs it and then attaches it to the inside of my black armband. "It goes on like this," she says. "Always hidden, but always there. Try not to lose it, and try not to show it to anyone."

"And if they ask, lie like a *hoohvak*," Ker adds, laughing with ease, as we both remember his awkward attempt at deception, the time I discovered his pin.

"Always there, *theoretically*," Erita says with a minor eye roll. "It's okay if you don't always remember to stick it on. They won't send *astra daimon* Correctors after you. . . . Half the time, I don't. I also lose these things every other month."

"Good to know there are replacements available," I say with amusement.

"Oh yeah," Erita laughs. "They're 3D printed on demand. Remind me to forward you the print design program, it's highly classified...."

Overhearing Erita, Tiliar chuckles, coming up to pat my shoulder. "As you can see, Kass, much of this *astra daimon* secret ritual stuff is pretty casual. It's the real actions that count. The heart-brother part is *real*." And he squeezes my arm with simple warmth.

Suddenly I feel my eyes blurring.

At this point, one after another, all the *astra daimon* start coming up to congratulate me. I'm told that, with a few exceptions and unforeseen obligations to be elsewhere, every single *daimon* is present here tonight, having come from various space outposts and stations all around the system and Atlantis itself, in order to attend my ceremony. That's why they needed such a large space—to fit hundreds of Pilots.

"So, Kass, were you surprised at this whole thing? Did you suspect anything?" Radanthet asks when it's his turn to swat me on my back.

"I was completely duped," I admit with chagrin. "Oalla told a good story and I fell for it."

"Ha! That's because you're a *bashtooh* fool!" Oalla exclaims. "I admit, I worked hard on getting the weird little details right —outrageous but just believable enough to get you out here, late in the evening and on a holiday. I can't believe you'd think I would ever, ever, *ever* let you endanger yourself like this, in a creepy abandoned warehouse, with no Imperial guards to protect you! Seriously? *Hoohvak!*"

"So, there's no party at your house?" I chuckle.

"*This* is the party!" She slaps me lightly on the side of my head then nudges my arm in mock anger. "The refreshments are in the back. See those tables? There's going to be music too—"

Just then, an older Pilot, tall and lean, with a copper-red cast to his skin approaches. He nods at me with a smile. "*Wixameret*, heart brother."

At first, he seems a stranger, but then suddenly I recognize him from my Fleet Cadet School days. . . .

I remember that fateful *kefarai* Combat *scolariat* when the four *astra daimon* visited us for the first time—the time I ended up sparring with Xelio and allowed him to win (back when he still hated me and I did not understand him). Of those four, this same *daimon* was the one with the Blue armband. And he was the one who singled me out and told me after class that I should apply to the SPC.

In those days we all thought of them as giants . . . I was that naïve boy with so many aspirations, and the astra daimon *towered in my imagination.*

"And now, here we are," the Pilot says, as if reading my mind. "Glad to have you with us, *daimon*. More than any of us, you've earned it."

"Nah, don't let it go to his head," Erita says, patting the top of my black armband. "He's already a big-shot—a national hero who gave his life for the Fleet, and the Imperial Crown Prince. Any more and he'll be a real stinking *shibet*."

Not sure why, but all this praise starts to affect me more than expected. I actually feel my face and neck burning with sudden embarrassment. "She's right, that's enough," I say to the Pilot whose name I still don't know (or don't quite recall, since I've no doubt that as a distinguished visitor he was formally introduced to our Cadet *scolariat* all those years ago, and in my stupid heightened state of hero worship I somehow missed it).

"Right about what? That you're a stinking *shibet?*" Xelio says, placing one arm around my shoulders and squeezing me to him in a parody of a romantic embrace, then pretending to nuzzle my throat. "Because, he definitely stinks. Um, what's this, some kind of musk, or floral?"

I laugh and shake my head, while disengaging from Xelio's hold with a practiced move. And then I turn back to the unnamed Pilot. "I want to thank you for your kind words to me, a long time ago. You visited my *scolariat* at Fleet Cadet School when I was just a *kefarai*. It meant a lot to me."

But the *daimon* continues to look at me, and his smile fades to a serious expression. "Thank me? After all those years? No, I must thank *you*."

He glances at my friends. "I meant every word; he earned this distinction more than anyone. If anyone is *astra daimon* in our generation, it is this man."

Then he turns again to me. "I was on that Rim Mission with you. If it hadn't been for your actions, I would've died at Ae-Leiterra."

There's a respectful pause as those nearest us overhear, and everyone focuses again on me, staring back and forth between the two of us.

Once again, I feel a stab of embarrassment at this extraordinary attention. But the *daimon* makes it easier for me by breaking the silence. "By the way, I don't think we've ever been directly introduced," he says. "I am Rumeiar Heru— honored to meet you."

At once I am curious. "Heru?" I ask. "As in, the Deshi Royal House?"

"Indeed, yes." The *daimon* makes an amused sound. "Though, nothing royal about me, just a very distant relative of the Pharikon."

Immediately my encyclopedic memory jumps to the roster of names of various royal and noble houses around the globe, all of which I had to memorize since childhood (in addition to other Princely things such as the geopolitical world map and endless Imperial protocols). At once I know this man, this *daimon* who made a difference for me all those years ago. . . .

My mind makes a few quick inferences and I place him. Rumeiar might be a distant Heru relative, but, due to the nature of several untimely deaths and the lack of direct living progeny in this ruling generation of the Royal House of New Deshret, he is actually fifth in line for the Deshi Throne.

UNTIMELY DEATHS. . . . Had I remained dead after Ae-Leiterra, my fragile sister Manala would have inherited the burden of the Imperial Throne here in *Atlantida.*

This grim thought snaps me back to the present—to my life-changing, difficult decision, and the continued perusal of the folded black armband lying before me in my cabin on ICS-2. At the same time, my experience with death's elusive nature torments my consciousness. And so, I give in once more, no matter how briefly, to the churning flood. . . .

DEATH . . .

It negates patterns, destroys information by disrupting its meaningful order.

Some say that order itself is divine.

And if order is divine, then we who are alive—who are ordered, complex energy constructs—are divine by our very fabric.

I don't mean that false divinity of the Kassiopei Dynasty, but the real spark of godhood in all of us: humans, sentient alien life forms, other living beings, lower animals, plants, microbial life. Even "inanimate" physical objects are alive on a quantum particle level.

The entire universe is alive, and it resonates, vibrating with energetic motion....

I THINK of the grand living universe and in my memories, I now dwell on a certain part of my recent chronology, filled to overflowing with life and events.

After becoming *astra daimon*, I continue my advancement in the SPC. The year 9766 that immediately follows finds me in a fiery rise in my career. In just a year and twelve months later— on Yellow Ghost Moon 25, 9767, the Eve of Golden Harvest—I earn the rank of Command Pilot in the Star Pilot Corps.

Yes, I'm a Command Pilot before I even turn sixteen. . . . Before my first Rite of Sacrifice (that fateful day is Blue Ghost Moon 21, 9767, exactly three months after my sixteenth birthday, on which I lose my physical innocence and discover the true depth of my Kassiopei lust).

But first—major events transpire in 9766. Hints and rumors of *them*, our ancient enemy, having found us once more are circulated by the *Atlantida* IEC (but the full truth possibly retained by my Imperial Father is yet to be seen), resulting in the Earth Mission announced to the public.

The Atlantean globe is in upheaval and must prepare for it. Immense ark-ships are built and equipped in orbit. Resources allocated, personnel chosen and trained, while nations haggle. . . . Advance surveillance missions (similar to the one on which Elikara and her father perished) return and bring us information about present-day conditions on Earth, and we begin to study their languages, primarily English.

And then approximately eight months after my CP rank, in view of my coming mission duties, I am somewhat surprised to find myself recommended by the international SPC command council as the replacement SPC Commander after the previous one retires.

I am sworn in as the SPC Commander on Red Amrevet 1 of the Year 9768 (and participate in my second Rite of Sacrifice on Yellow Amrevet 21, 9768, nine months after the first Rite).

In just eight months after becoming Commander, on Yellow Ghost Moon 13, 9768, the Fleet departs on the Earth Mission—so that I have to name an acting SPC Commander in my absence (Nomarch Evandros) and step down a rank to be the Command Pilot in the Imperial Fleet—my current designation.

Life, seething with events, delimited by chronology. I understand it better when I view its multidimensional plurality through my filter of knowing death.

THE UNIVERSE IS one complex living fabric of immortality, punctuated by death.

All of us, separate, disparate entities, exist for the simple reason that the "divine living fabric" (pure energy and light) can be periodically ripped apart (smashed and torn at the sub-atomic quantum level) by the death process, which is nothing more than multi-dimensional manipulation of space-time.

During that "rip," the linear continuity of the One Universal Sentience is temporarily disrupted, *negated*—before the divine fabric once more closes in on itself and self-heals the damage ... resumes immortality.

And that's how all of us individual entities are created—we exist between "rips," each of our lives a segment torn out of infinity. . . .

Death transforms all of us temporarily into "shreds" of our immortal selves. It grants pause to our personal timelines and permits entropy and chaos.

The ultimate gift is indeed oblivion—a respite from the burden of immortality. . . .

Death allows the Immortal Divine to "go on holiday"—to separate from *itself* and *forget* . . . in order to create and maintain the multi-dimensionality of the universe.

SUDDENLY I'M PLUNGED BACK to those early days on Earth during Qualification, when I narrowly escaped death for the second time. Once again, I survive a damaged falling shuttle (. . . shades of Ae-Leiterra . . .) while my friends and colleagues who are in the other transport that explodes, do not.

Moments after takeoff from the RQC-3 airfield, my transport shuttle malfunctions. It begins spinning out of control and falling. Despite my best efforts to reestablish flight, I'm pummeled by g-forces, flung about the interior of the shuttle itself. My safety harness prevents me from the worst kind of injury; still, I lose consciousness. . . .

Instead of dying, I wake up in the med tech unit, miraculously rescued by *someone*, perfectly healed once again by our advanced medical tech. Oalla and Xelio are there to greet me, their expressions grim and terrible. That's when I learn about the other shuttle's explosion—likely caused by Earth sabotage—and the resulting deaths.

Tiliar. . . .

I remember the scorching grief and red-hot fury overcoming me. . . .

Tiliar Vahad, my friend and *astra daimon* heart-brother was in that other shuttle. With him were two other excellent Pilots, Chiar Nuridat and the young Felekamen Gori. Both with so much promise, all their lives and careers ahead of them.

But, Tiliar . . . *no!*

Stop—don't think.

Even now, more than a year later, fury returns to strike me with its implacable force, like ocean surf against cliffs, railing in futility at the injustice of permanent loss.

One of the last things that Tiliar tells me (as we leave the RQC-3 airfield hangar, and pause briefly before heading for the two separate shuttles) is that he discovered he really likes Earth raspberries. Supposedly, the Gebi figured out that the taste of raspberries is like the taste of space itself, and he had to verify it for himself.

"Space has a taste?" Felekamen asks in surprise, widening his brown eyes, and Chiar merely chuckles, low and throaty.

"Yes, sort of—due to the chemical molecule they call ethyl formate," Tiliar explains. "It is often found in space, and it also happens to give raspberries their flavor. Sometimes, the Gebi even use it as an artificial flavor."

"Artificial flavor? The Gebi are rather strange," Chiar says wisely, adjusting one of the ties on his long, segmented tail. "The kinds of things they eat, no wonder. . . . At least those berries are somewhat healthy. But otherwise, very little nutritional value in their so-called junk food. Just to think, that's the stuff they are serving the Candidates in their meal halls."

"Not entirely their fault," Tiliar says after a thoughtful pause. "Earth's soil has been severely depleted of nutrients due to poor farming practices and insufficient amount of organic matter and animal waste being recycled back into the ecosystem. Everything they grow in soil these days is deficient, hence, junk food. Highly processed, too. They should try hydroponics."

As soon as Tiliar mentions hydroponics (his field of expertise) I remember something that needs to be done and ask him to run some data analysis with Anu Vei when we get back to ICS-2.

"Will do," my friend replies in his usual comfortable manner. "But first, sorry, have to use the interstellar comms to make a quick scheduled call to my family back on *Atlantida*. Promised to call my sister Mara. It's been a while, and my turn finally came up to use the comms equipment."

"Of course," I say to him, "That's priority one, do that. Give my best to your sister and the others."

"Will do, Kass," Tiliar says, turning from me for the last time. "See you and Vei at the CCO in half an hour."

I see his calm, reliable, infinitely relatable face now, seared in my memory, that last motion of turning away in profile . . . And then I briefly watch his solid figure retreating toward the *varqood* shuttle that will bring about his death.

The other two—I don't really remember them as well, in those last moments. I believe Chiar gives me a casual hand wave, while rubbing his forehead tiredly after our long workday, and Felekamen salutes. That's when I turn away from all of them, and go to my own shuttle.

I am not going to see them ever again.

THEIR DEATHS ARE QUICK, possibly instant, in the fiery explosion. Logic tells me it must be so (it had to have been a quicker death than the one I experienced at Ae-Leiterra), but my grief blows up and rages with the same explosive intensity. However, since I'm a master of outward control, I internalize it to the point that I become hard and implacable as ice, in order to contain it.

I allow myself a brief softening as I notify Tiliar's family via interstellar comms (ah, Mara Vahad . . . I'll never forget the light going out of her eyes as I tell her about her brother . . .), and then I do the same thing for Felekamen and Chiar—since the grim duty of informing their loved ones falls upon me, their commanding officer. The less said about it, the better.

But my grief must have an outlet. I set it loose upon the entire Candidate population of RQC-3.

First, I bring in the Correctors. The investigations begin. And then I torment the Candidates in each Quadrant by forcing them all through a merciless Er-Du training routine at the Arena Commons.

This is when I encounter *her* again—the girl with the clear gaze. It happens under the most unexpected circumstances, and this time I cannot contain myself. My rage translates into an emotional *connection* to her.

This connection . . . it's brought about by an honorable act of stupid courage, even as this girl defies me. In order to help a fellow Candidate, she goes against my direct order given to the entire Yellow Quadrant that's presently being punished by me.

Normally I would respect and understand and encourage such a thing.

But not this time. Cold fury makes me implacable, hard and cruel. And it occurs to me later that in this I am, no matter how briefly, not much different from my Imperial Father. . . .

And yet, even underneath my anger, beyond the dark pit of grief in which I drown, on a deep level of the soul, I *know* precisely what she is doing, I see the rightness . . . enough to admire it.

I vividly recall how I walk between the rows of Candidates performing Er-Du forms with sloppy, fearful compulsion.

"Halt!" I roar at them. "Stop, and assume Floating Swan!"

I pace through their motionless rows, observing these same young Gebi now awkwardly frozen in the Floating Swan Form. There is only the sound of my boots striking the floor, and my Logos voice. "Shame and disgrace! You are not worthy of being called *Candidates* much less *Atlanteans.* You move like a herd of Earth cattle—broken, weak, useless! How badly out of shape are you, considering you are teenagers? An old man on Atlantis can move his dying carcass better than you!"

Each time I see a particularly egregious example, I tell the Candidate to step forward and receive punishment.

"You! Take one step forward! You! And you! Step forward! You! Step forward! You! *Move!*"

And having chosen my scapegoats, I say, "Those whom I called forward, will now *stand on one foot* until I tell you otherwise. If you set your other foot down, you will have to repeat, for twice the time. *Now, stand on your right foot!*"

I make *them* the example, because I must, because one or more of them is guilty of the murder of my heart brother and two others. . . . In those moments I feel an irrational, generalized hatred toward all Gebi. Before me is an ocean of stupid, selfish, ungrateful, self-destructive, malicious human garbage . . . *but no, they're just kids. . . .*

Soon, the great arena space fills with more and more thusly punished Candidates. It's an ordeal of endurance. Periodically I tell them to switch to the other foot to give them a tiny break, and then keep going. Meanwhile I order the rest of the arena to resume their Forms Cycle exercises.

I hear them grumble, and, as an additional punishment, order one boy to not only stand on one foot but to jump up and down as he's doing it.

And then I see *her*. The girl has stepped forward on her own, volunteering herself for the punishment. . . . Why? Apparently she's holding the hand of another girl—one who's actually being punished next to her—and helping her to keep balance. It's revealed later that there's a good reason for it; the other girl has a foot injury.

I stop. At first all I can see is that this female is *not* one of the Candidates I singled out for punishment, and her poor attempt at deception infuriates me even further.

And then, as I look closer, I recognize her.

She is that girl with the fierce clarity of gaze, the impossibly real, intimate, blue eyes full of *something* for which I have no words, but which is an aspect of truth.

But in that moment, I have no mercy.

"You!" I say to her in my cold rage. "What are you doing?"

She continues to stand on one foot, staring straight ahead and not looking at me. Her fingers are still in contact with the other girl's hand.

I pause, doing nothing for several long heartbeats of strange focus. The world narrows in on us . . . her and me.

Nothing else exists. . . .

"Look at me . . ." I say, hearing my own voice grow quieter, but not any less deadly. "I *said*, what are you doing?"

Slowly she turns her head a small fraction—to meet my gaze. And it feels as if something strikes me hard in the gut, a firebolt.

"I . . . don't know . . ." she whispers.

I slam a shield of perfect control over my intensity, masking my response to her. *Those eyes. . . .*

"You what? You don't *know*?" My Logos voice destroys her.

"I am sorry, I don't—"

"I did not tell you to step forward and stand on one foot. So, what are you doing?"

"I—must've misunderstood."

At this point, my anger is such that I am close to exploding.

Somehow, I maintain my blank exterior, and take a step toward her. Slowly I look her over, top to bottom. I see her slim, well-proportioned, tall form, the determined stance her body takes—no slumped shoulders this time. And she continues to hold the other girl's hand.

I disengage my gaze—almost regretfully—and turn to look at the girl she is helping, who indeed appears to be unwell.

There is perfect silence in the arena, except for a few people shifting their feet, and the lonely sound of one boy jumping up and down, his foot laboriously striking the floor.

I ignore all of it and return my attention to the strangely remarkable girl who is defying me. It's time I learned more about her, starting with her identity.

"Your name, Candidate," I ask, training the full force of my gaze upon her.

"Gwen Lark."

Her name, so this is her name . . . Gwen Lark.

I watch her, as the moment appears to extend. Again, that strange sensation of slipping away into a narrow reality where there are only the two of us and nothing else exists. . . . A super focus.

"Do you make it a habit to willfully *misunderstand* instructions?" I ask, allowing sarcasm to radiate from me.

The girl whose name is Gwen Lark appears to be caught in my stare, as if ensnared in a trap. I can almost see the racing pulse in her throat.

"No . . . only sometimes," she replies. Her voice initially sounds young and frightened, but then it too seems to gain strength.

"And is there a reason you are holding hands with the Candidate next to you?" Merciless sarcasm darkens all my reason and turns my voice into a sharp blade. I'm actually enjoying the fear in her. I can almost taste it, and it makes me *wild. . . .*

She takes a deep breath and glances at the other female. I notice, the sickly girl barely manages to keep her eyes open, while rivulets of sweat pour down her temples.

"She is hurt," Gwen Lark says. "She cannot stand like that on her right leg. . . . At least not for much longer."

"I see. So you think you are helping her?"

"I *am*—helping her." This is where her voice becomes resonant.

There is a pause.

"You are *cheating*." I say harshly. "The consequence for such action is Disqualification. For *both* of you—"

"No!" Gwen exclaims, letting go of the other girl's fingers as if burned, and appears ready to cry. "No, *she* had nothing to do with it! It was all my idea! Please, she really *is* hurt!"

"—and punishment for disobeying direct orders is also Disqualification," I continue in an implacable tone, ignoring her outburst. My voice has grown deceptively soft, serpentine— and I have no doubt that in that moment I'm terrifying . . . as I intend to be.

Gwen stands, still balancing on one foot, breathing in shallow rapid gasps, while her eyes are filling with liquid.

Ignore those hurting eyes . . . show no compassion.

In that exact moment, the injured girl next to Gwen

collapses without a sound. She goes limp, passing out, and falls on the floor.

Gwen gasps and reacts immediately. She crouches before her and feels the girl's head.

"Candidates, halt!" My voice is still hard and impassive, but my rage has broken. "All of you, stop and you may put both feet down."

Hearing my command, at once Oalla blows a whistle. The crowd of Candidates responds, and there's a shuffle of many feet.

Gwen Lark continues holding the girl's forehead. Moments later the girl regains consciousness. Keruvat approaches and squats down next to the two of them. He checks the girl's pulse, then moves behind her, and together he and Gwen raise the girl up into a sitting position on the floor.

I can hear Gwen whispering to Keruvat. "Please. . . . She really needs a doctor!"

"No . . . I am all right," the injured girl speaks up in a barely audible voice. She manages to get up slowly with their help, and stands looking dazed.

To her credit, she then attempts to once again stand on one leg. She must have missed hearing me issue the halt command when she was unconscious on the floor.

"You," I tell her, keeping my tone implacable, even though —now that I know her condition—I pity her. "For the rest of this class, you are excused. You are also excused from today's Agility Training. Go back to your Dorm and see the doctor."

"Am I—Disqualified?" she whispers. Her stoic brown eyes reveal a world of despair.

"No. Not *today*," I tell her, as my regret over this girl's condition starts to rise.

Then I hear Gwen Lark's shuddering breath followed by a brave question, "What about me?"

I return my attention to her, and again our gazes lock together. Immediately, something is happening, a searing intensity of *contact*.

But no, there is no contact, *what nonsense. . . .*

I'm merely still worked up over doling out the mass punishment. This is just me coming down from the boiling anger back into my more sensible state of controlled grief.

And yet . . . why is it that Gwen Lark appears to have difficulty moving, and is taking shallow breaths? Why? *Bashtooh*, it's because she's asked me a terrifying question and I still haven't replied.

I wait another heartbeat, intentionally tormenting her.

And then I say, "You—I still have not decided."

The rows of Candidates have fallen into perfect silence, watching in fear and suspense.

With my peripheral vision I can see Keruvat glancing at me. Meanwhile Oalla is extremely still and quiet.

In that moment Xelio approaches. He leans in and tells me in *Atlanteo*, "Kass . . . trust me, you don't want to Disqualify this girl."

"Why not?" I ask.

"Because she is far too clever to dismiss."

"Being too clever is what got her into this situation." I hold back a more sarcastic retort.

"You need to hear what she did in my Combat class," Xel says to me with an unexpected hint of a smile.

And this is when I first learn about the Shoelace incident. Xelio quickly gives me the details. In short, Gwen Lark ended up last in a weapons draw, found herself without a cord weapon and, to avoid a demerit, *made* her own on the spot. She pulled out her own shoelaces from her sneakers, tied them together into a single "cord" and presented it to Xel, which impressed him to no end.

As I listen, it becomes clear that I need to reserve my judgment when it comes to this female Candidate.

And so, I look back at her now as she stands in terrible suspense. I glance down at her feet and those infamous sneakers. Surprisingly, I feel a wave of amusement break past my grief—amusement which I stifle at once—but at this point all my anger retreats completely.

I decide right then that *I am not done* with her.

"Candidate Lark, for the moment, you are *not* Disqualified," I say, watching her with my steady gaze that has become a familiar mask. "However, you will report here later tonight during Homework Hour, for disciplinary action."

I barely motion with my head in the direction of the raised platform deck in the back of the stadium. "Be on that deck, on time, at 8:00 PM sharp, to receive further instructions. That is all for now."

I look away from her. And just like that, I force myself to think of her as *nothing*.

Clever or not, she is insignificant. Just another public example to be made of. Except, this time, there will be far less anger on my part and more of my usual rational sense and control. . . .

Meanwhile, the injured girl who had collapsed moments earlier leaves her row and walks away slowly and stiffly, yet somehow exhibiting remarkable dignity, to seek medical treatment. All of us briefly watch her retreating back. Xelio in particular seems to linger, watching her movements with a serious expression.

Not wasting another moment, I pull myself back into my command role and resume pacing the rows of Candidates.

Once more, my voice rises to a Logos level of focus as I command the arena: "Candidates! Resume your Forms and Examples! Show me First Form, Floating Swan! The rest of you who are Examples, stand on your right foot!"

Even as I speak, I think of what will happen later tonight when Gwen Lark comes to receive her punishment.

$$\sim$$

I KNOW NOW that *death* is intimately connected to *memory*.

Memory is the uninterrupted fabric of consciousness, a linear record of space-time, a single vibrating energetic string. It can be paused and its resonance silenced.

This brief interruption is death's oblivion.

Otherwise, memory is immortal.

Eventually the entity-string reforms, resumes vibrating again, as it must . . . is interrupted again . . . again and again, infinitely. And those phase states in between, those thresholds, musical interruptions, create the rhythm, melody, and fabric of the universe . . . of all the universes.

Death is the *drumbeat*.

$$\sim$$

IN THE HERE AND NOW, on board ICS-2 headed home to Atlantis, I continue to focus on my black armband. Stilled in that meditative, thoughtful state, I follow the next set of memories in my deepening experience with Gwen Lark.

Incidentally—I tell myself all of this is necessary in the

course of my reasoning and logical analysis, my looming decision in regard to her. Truth is, I find these memories pleasurable. Yes, there, I admit to myself that I derive a peculiar pleasure in every moment of remembering even my smallest interactions with her, every step of this strange compelling journey my mind takes.

And so, back to my recollection. . . .

After the "clever" girl undergoes her ridiculous punishment in the arena (because I'm a *chazuf*, I make her stand on one foot or the other for half an hour while I watch her from my office monitor) she arrives upstairs at my office.

Still being a *chazuf*, I take my time working the control center consoles and make her wait. Meanwhile she chats with Candidate Blayne Dubois whom she apparently knows and who is also in my office. When I finally turn and give my attention to both of them, the girl flushes with anxiety as soon as our gazes meet. In fact, she turns such a bright shade of red that I momentarily pity her and pretend not to see—and then our interaction begins.

First, she asks if she is to be disciplined further. And for some reason I find myself toying with her a while longer.

"You found it insufficient?" I ask, amusing myself wickedly at her expense—except, *bashtooh*, what's wrong with me? "If the activity you've performed just now in the arena is not enough, then I can accommodate you with more. Would you like to go back on that platform and repeat?"

"Oh, no!" she exclaims.

I relent and explain that she's here to assist Candidate Dubois in his special training in Limited Mobility Forms.

Blayne Dubois is wheelchair-bound, and I want him to have a fighting chance in the cruel process of Qualification. The boy is extraordinary in his character and determination, having made it this far. Furthermore, his initial Pre-

Qualification test results reveal significant talent in multiple areas that would greatly benefit *Atlantida*. There's just something about him that makes me want to champion him and help him succeed. And hoverboard fighting skills are the only thing I can give him without crossing the line of favoritism.

And so, I start the lesson by showing Blayne the basic LM Forms while Gwen assists by holding the hoverboard.

When it's done, I step back, feeling actual sweat on my forehead from the nicely intensive workout. "Good work, both of you," I say.

In that moment, I notice that, for some reason, Gwen Lark seems to be looking at the exact spot on the side of my head which was injured during the shuttle incident. She glances away quickly, which I find curious, but dismiss it as merely an example of my own careful and sometimes overly suspicious tendency to question others' actions. Besides, although the med techs healed all my recent injuries, something might still be visible; possibly, there's faint, leftover scar tissue. . . .

No longer staring at me, Gwen looks over at the command station consoles, while Blayne makes it to his wheelchair with the help of the hoverboard and sits down, hard. He's sweat-covered, his arms trembling from our sparring workout. I feel for him, but right now he has to work twice as hard to stay competitive, so this is for his own good.

There's a brief pause, while I pick up a towel to wipe my own sweat.

And then Gwen asks another blunt question that, intentionally or not, gets a rise out of me. "Why don't you let Blayne borrow the hoverboard all the time? He could get around so much easier if he had it—"

Her words fade into silence.

Still holding the towel, I turn around and look at her. "Your suggestion is noted. Unfortunately, it is out of the question."

"But why? It would be such a good thing!"

Bashtooh, this girl either has no sense that she is challenging me, a High Command ranking officer, or she doesn't seem to care. . . . I find it refreshingly astounding and also quite annoying.

"Candidate Lark, are you questioning me?" I say, after an initial moment of amazement.

She gulps, possibly struggling with her own common sense while choosing how to respond. And then, unbelievably, she continues to push back at me. "Yes . . . because there's just no good reason why you should say no! I mean, it makes no sense why it shouldn't be allowed, just a single hoverboard—"

I look at her in disbelief, drop the towel on the nearest surface, then take a step toward her. Something *wild* once again rises inside me, and before I can hold myself back, I ask, "Are you always like this?"

"Oh, yeah, she is," Blayne says, shaking his head in mild disgust. He pushes hair from his face and looks down wearily. He appears unsurprised.

Good to know.

Gwen whirls around, and glares at Blayne. "Oh, yeah? Well, considering I'm doing this for *you*, the least thing you could do is shut up!"

"Oh, jeez. . . ." The boy puts his head down and passes his hand through his hair. "Please don't do me any favors!"

At once the girl's righteous energy is gone, and she appears startled, even sad.

"I am sorry," she says, taking a deep breath. It's as if she realizes at last that she has gone too far.

Here, I begin to get a deeper glimpse of her nature. I note

that she is impulsive and meddlesome in general (even if it's for the best kind of reasons), trying to fix things that are none of her concern and frankly beyond her control.

"Look," she adds, still addressing Blayne with anxious sympathy, "I really am sorry, and I know it is not my business to press, but it seems to me the *logical* thing to do, a perfect solution to a *logistics problem*, and maybe that's why it drives me nuts to see a perfectly good tool not being used in a capacity where it can truly help—"

As she babbles, I look at her in continued amazement, forgetting to mask my response. Even now, although she's speaking to Blayne, she is still pushing back and *contradicting* me.

And so, I interrupt her tirade. "*Enough.* You have expressed yourself, and because you are a civilian and don't know better, I have allowed it. And now, you will no longer speak on this subject unless you would like to be disciplined again. Is that understood, Candidate?"

She nods, with widened eyes. "Yes."

Her eyes . . . they are so guileless, so full of clarity. . . . Bashtooh! *Stop noticing her eyes.*

Clamping down my own emotional response, angry at myself, I smile at her—the kind of controlled smile that falls in the repertoire of my public mask. At full strength, I've been told, it can be terrifying—dark, sarcastic, confident, *Imperial.*

"Good," I say. "Now, because you *are* in an unusual position of not knowing better, and you've indeed asked me a logical question, I am going to answer you. But only this once."

I pause, examining her, watching for the smallest reaction.

Surprisingly, she remains still and silent, not giving me *anything.*

"The main reason I cannot permit hoverboard use outside

the classrooms and training halls is because we cannot afford to let even one orichalcum-based piece of technology to go missing and fall into the wrong hands, and potentially be stolen from this compound. Yes, I know Candidate Dubois is responsible and would never intentionally misplace or misuse the hoverboard. However, he sleeps at night, and cannot be vigilant around the clock."

She briefly glances at Blayne, who in turn is listening carefully.

"The second reason," I continue, "is that there can be no favoritism displayed in the process of Qualification. If I let Dubois fly around on this thing, even with his legitimate need-based reason, I would set a precedent. Other Candidates would make rightful demands to be allowed equal use of hoverboards, and that's something we cannot do. There are other reasons, but these are the main ones, and I hope— Candidate Lark—that I have *satisfied* your need for a *logical* explanation."

I grow silent, and watch her. After all the solid evidence in support of my argument I've given her, is she convinced?

"Yes, thank you," she says in a subdued voice. And yet, she doesn't appear meek but rather thoughtful.

Sufficient, for now. . . . I allow my mind to ease.

"Good," I say, "Now, you are both dismissed for today, and I will see you both back here tomorrow night, at the beginning of your Homework Hour. We'll work from eight to eight thirty. In the meantime, you are not to speak of the nature of this activity to anyone, because again, I want no Candidate speculation about preferential treatment. If asked, you may say you are meeting with Instructors to get help with your homework."

Blayne nods, and starts pushing his wheelchair to the door. "Thanks for your time, Mr. Kass," he says.

"Command Pilot Kass is the proper address," I correct him, but without reproach.

"Sorry, Command Pilot Kass," Blayne mutters. "Thank you for all the work you put in with me. I am sorry to be taking up your time—"

"No problem." I nod at him and my lips curve slightly. This time, my smile is sincere, not my controlled public demeanor.

Not sure what exactly Gwen Lark notices in that genuine moment, but she appears to be looking at me closely, as if recognizing that something is different in my expression.

"If it's permitted to ask," she says, lingering at the door after holding it open for Blayne. "Why am I here? Why not someone else more suitable to help him train? There are plenty of big strong guys in our Dorm who would do a better job."

I'm already heading back to my command station—the area of my office with the observation consoles and plural surveillance screens containing information not intended for their eyes. It's been a long day, and to be honest, I'm tired, and still not at my full energy levels after my serious injury. However, the fact that she's still here, causes me to pause. *What else does she expect of me now?*

"I could tell you it's to keep an eye on you, Lark," I reply in a voice that's as bland as I can make it. "But really, there isn't a particularly exciting explanation."

And then something cruel and contrary makes me continue: "Don't flatter yourself, you're not that interesting. The simple fact is, you happened to be here already, and you are sufficiently up to the task. As your Instructors say, you might have something—some quirk, some potential. So now, by all means, *show me* you are not merely an unremarkable teenager with an inability to keep her mouth shut, and with poor impulse control. Prove me wrong. Now—dismissed."

And I turn away from her, cool and implacable—but not before catching the wounded expression of her eyes. They remain remarkably clear, but now they're also filled with outrage.

She leaves, and I don't remember the events of the rest of that night.

Instead, all I recall is my inner turmoil and sense of confusion at my own rampant *emotions* and my own words.

Inexplicably and unnecessarily, I've just informed her that she's "not that interesting" and "unremarkable." And yet, by declaring these things I've forced myself to admit that my subconscious mind has seriously considered those attributes in regard to her.

By my own logic, the fact that I'm even dwelling on her attributes negates the validity of my argument.

Logic can go *varqood* itself.

By calling her uninteresting I've made her very *interesting* indeed. And by calling her unremarkable, I've just sealed my own doom.

So . . . this is where it starts.

THE EVENTS of the following days roll into one strange, agonizing succession. At some point we return to ICS-2 and hold a private memorial for the dead. All the senior officers, my *daimon sen-i-senet* and I, and any other crew members who had a bond with them—all of us stationed on board this command vessel, participate in the ceremony where we sing our heart brother Tiliar into eternity, and we sing the same for Felekamen and Chiar.

Since their bodies have not been recovered, there are no

wreaths to lay upon them, no flowers or personal belongings to lay with them for the burning.

They have burned already . . . their remains are dust in Earth's atmosphere . . . with time, falling to the surface, becoming one with our ancient home world.

Our songs therefore fill an empty Resonance Chamber, and our own living bodies stand in for theirs. As we mourn, our voices fade also, stilling. Only memory remains and the sad task of boxing up the personal things in their cabins for the long journey home.

Then, we return to our mission duties. Qualification training is happening even while Correctors continue investigations into the deaths. My own damaged shuttle—what remains of it—is examined, and the techs find a suspicious empty slot and a missing micro-component in the drive system to corroborate a malicious act of tampering. Further investigation leads to delivery trucks employed at RQC-3. One of the missing shuttle navigation chips is located after a search of the trucks before they leave the compound, while another chip presumably taken from the other shuttle is yet to be recovered and is still unaccounted for.

This botched attempt at smuggling the components out of RQC-3 gives the Correctors a lead and connects this activity to any of several pro-Earth and anti-Atlantis terrorist organizations. It's assumed they have a cell operating at the compound. What are their motives? Possibly, assassination of High Command officers such as myself. Or more likely, obtaining our hardware for Earth's benefit, a clumsy move to reverse engineer and learn our advanced technology.

Meanwhile, I supervise all these investigations, full of simmering anger and grief, even as my thoughts continue to return to a certain female Candidate. Minor details about her suddenly become important. . . . I learn that she has three other siblings, all Pre-Qualified, all here at the RQC-3. I also see her with a boy, Candidate Logan Sangre. But these details do not distract me from the grim duties at hand.

Soon enough, arrests are made. Two of the arrested Candidates are directly linked to terrorist groups Terra Patria and the Sunset Alliance. The third—a girl in Yellow Dorm Eight, found with the second stolen navigation chip in her pocket—happens to be a friend of Gwen Lark. After Candidate Laronda Aimes is taken into custody, Gwen and another of her Dorm friends arrive the next morning, demanding that Candidate Aimes is innocent.

By then, we indeed establish that Aimes is not the guilty party, and I'm about to release her. However, for some crazy reason, I permit Gwen Lark to see me in person to present her case. I actually look forward to seeing her rant.

And then . . . everything falls apart. Lark raises her voice, and the lab equipment flags her as a resonance signature match tied directly to my shuttle *interior*—to the control panel components. In other words, she had to have been there, *inside* my shuttle—and not just in the crowd of bystanders during my ground rescue.

Because yes, according to limited surveillance around the airfield (most of the wired cameras and sensitive nano-cams were damaged by the sonic blast of the explosion) and RQC-3 staff eyewitnesses, reportedly she was already there near the shuttle when the rescuers found me—probably sticking around to make sure I was dead. Or worse—she could've been there to finish me off, interrupted only when the guards and medics arrived on the scene.

In that moment of realization, my anger and grief explode. All my emotions are now oceanic in violence, fueled by profound *regret* that *this girl* of all people is the one who tried to harm me.

Now it makes sense why she was staring at the side of my head earlier during our LM training with Dubois. She must've known exactly where I was injured. She *saw* me hurt and unconscious.

All this time, she's lied to me, has been playing me.

She's not an innocent but a lying *sha*.

And so, furious and insane from so much conflicted emotion, I detain her, and have her put into a prison cell.

Then I send in the Correctors to question her while I watch from the other room.

And that's when things really escalate.

THE CORRECTORS' line of questioning pushes Gwen Lark to admit why she was there *inside* my shuttle.

The girl arms herself with her artful semblance of innocence and claims that she was there to *rescue* me from the shuttle. Even more outrageous, she shamelessly insists that she used voice commands to safely bring down my falling shuttle.

Ignoring the latter idiocy, the Correctors confront her with the logical inconsistency of her being capable of carrying my considerably larger, heavy body out of the shuttle.

"Yes!" she gasps, acting her part so well that now tears begin running down her face. "And no, I did not *carry* him, I dragged him! Do *not*—do not put words in my mouth! I pulled and dragged him outside the best I could, yes! And he was heavy, yes, but I wasn't going to just leave him—"

In that moment my raging pain knows no bounds. . . . I need to act, which means I must take over the questioning. And so, I leave my observation chamber and storm into the interrogation room.

"*Enough*," I say in a hard voice, looking at the Correctors. "Outside, both of you, *now*. I will handle the rest of this *interview*."

There is a pause. The Correctors then incline their heads in acquiescence and depart the room.

As soon as the door shuts behind them, I turn to her. I slam both hands on the table, and stand, looking down at her.

I am now a demon. Her demon. And I will make her pay.

She trembles. Tears pour down her face in a torrent, and she takes a few shuddering gasps of air.

"Tell me *exactly* what you did," I command in my Logos voice, soft and precise and devastating.

She turns up her eyes at me. They are wide and motionless, and the blue of her irises seems lighter in hue somewhat, from all her weeping.

Her expression is so truthful and clear, so genuine, righteous . . . No!

She raises one hand, clenched into a white-knuckled fist, to wipe her reddened nose and cheeks with the back of it. Her lips are puffy and swollen, appearing fuller, and for some reason I look at them. . . .

"What I *did?*" she says, and her voice breaks. "I hauled your damn, bloody, passed-out ass out of that burning shuttle, is what I did!"

I watch her, the curves of her cheeks, the delicate shape of her chin, the line of her neck . . . keeping my mask of control, never allowing myself to blink. Several seconds pass, while conflicting thoughts race through my mind in a tornado.

"Tell me how you found me," I ask at last. It will prove

nothing, of course, but I want to hear her say it. "Where was I in the shuttle?"

"You were in a chair. In some kind of harness. You were slumped over."

"And how was I hurt?"

She stares at me, and her gaze automatically slides to the place on the side of my head where my healed injury used to be. *Ah, there it is, her admission.*

"Your head," she says. "It was on that side, and there was a lot of blood."

"Where? Show me," I persist, because I must hear her say it —all of it.

She hesitates.

My hand slams the table, hard. *"Show me!"*

She partially rises from her seat and extends her right hand, moving trembling fingers to point to the spot.

My long hair, worn loose today, happens to fall forward as I lean over her . . . and so she touches it lightly, *feels* it.

"Here . . ." she says in a voice that's become almost gentle. "And here. . . . There was so much blood, and it stained all of your face, and your hair too."

A *firebolt* strikes me, at her touch.

Bashtooh!

It's the faintest contact possible—her fingers barely graze the long tendrils of my hair—but the electric current it sends down my scalp is a sudden shock.

As the firebolt passes down my body, I feel a twitch in my genitals.

Rawah bashtooh!

I blink. Just once. Because, what can I do? My body is betraying me simultaneously above and *below*. . . . My damned *varqooi* has decided to come alive, and I'm aware of the sudden heat down there.

Accursed Kassiopei lust, surfacing at the worst time possible. . . . Normally I'm much better at keeping it under check, but this—this is ridiculous.

As a result, I can barely maintain sufficient control over my demeanor and breath, over my mouth, keeping a hard, implacable line.

She has no idea what's happening to me. . . .

It has to stop.

I gather myself, slamming walls over my senses. And I focus on her role instead of her actual person. I remind myself she's a skilled deceiver with a hostile Gebi agenda.

"Why should I believe you?" I say, because I must continue the interrogation. "Why should anything you tell me exonerate you?"

"Because it's the truth!" Her response is immediate and organic. Again, her expression evokes instant sympathy while conveying such righteousness.

Deceiver. . . .

I narrow my eyes in fury. "Oh, it's *truth*, you claim? How well you are playing me even now—have been playing me all along, with your little innocent act!"

She stops sniffling and her mouth falls open in anger. Great acting skills.

But we're done playing, and I'm laying it out in the open. I continue speaking, my face hovering above hers as I lean in yet closer, full of dark sarcasm. "It becomes clear now, how you've insinuated yourself with all the Instructors. . . . Such a clever little teacher's pet! So creative, so many bright ideas! Sweet little girl with such pretty earnest eyes . . . such sweet rosy lips . . . except when they're spouting pure bullshit!"

These unfortunate *shar-ta-haak* words just tumble out of me. . . . The things I'm saying right now—*bashtooh*, yes, they're sarcastic and intentionally merciless—but not sure why I'm bringing up some of these details, such as her facial features. . . .

Did I just admit that I've noticed her well-formed mouth? That her lips are "sweet" and "rosy" and that I've been staring at them all this time?

Enough, I need to contain myself.

She makes a stifled sound, her expression a helpless mix of outrage and terror. Such a farce.

I want to destroy her.

I step around the table and suddenly pull her up out of her chair. I grip her bare wrist, feeling its slim fragility—and the sensation is followed by another sudden electric shock of physical contact. Her jacket slides down and ends up halfway off her shoulders as I hold her there with my other hand, my rough fingers digging into her bare, soft skin, bruising her shoulder, its pristine smoothness. . . .

She stumbles backwards, away from me, and I push her hard against the wall, so that I'm breathing into her face. A madness overcomes me, and my heart pounds abnormally. I feel the flush of heat traveling from my head and spreading all throughout my body, especially down below. . . . Again, my *varqooi* is twitching.

Rawah bashtooh. . . .

"Tell me, *Gwen Lark*, what group are you affiliated with?" I speak, focusing on the precision of my words now, the Logos voice cutting into her—all the while attempting to control my physical response. "Terra Patria or the Sunset Alliance? Or wait, let me guess, neither—for you are far too clever to be a pawn of such narrow-minded small-scale idiots. So I am guessing you are working with some bigger fish. So tell me, which is it?"

"I am not!" She gasps, half-turning her face away as my ragged breath washes over her cheek, her neck. "I am not working with anyone!"

My grip on her shoulder hardens, in tandem with my body (my *varqooi* is now rigid), and so my grip becomes steel. At the same time, without realizing it, I also squeeze her wrist—until she cries out in pain.

Like a serpent I hiss in her ear, "Who trained you?"

"No one! No one trained me! Stop it! Let *go* of me!"

The echo of her resonant voice rings inside my head.

Let go of me.

As if burned, I release my hold and step back away from her. I'm breathing hard.

What is wrong with me? What kind of dark sha *impulses are these? What have I done? Enough . . . I've crossed a line.*

Even if she is, most likely, the enemy, she is skinny and fragile and pitiful. She is young and human. And as of yet, there's no concrete, undeniably *verified* proof of her crimes.

I still myself, breathing mindfully, slowing my heartbeats with a force of will. Moments later, I'm sufficiently composed. I straighten, and my facial expression closes up into its proper blank mask.

Cold as ice, I stand watching her.

She, too, strands up straight, moves away from the wall, and pulls up her jacket back over her T-shirt and her smooth, bare arms. She glares at me.

"What can I say to make you believe I did nothing wrong?" she says in a tone of despair. "What kind of proof do you need?"

I am implacable now, completely in control, mind and body.

"There is nothing you can do or tell me now that I will believe ever again," I say. "Not until I can discover hard undeniable facts that point otherwise. Can you give me such facts?"

"I—I don't know. I don't even know what you're talking about."

"Ah. . . . Then, keep playing," I say softly.

"Holy lord!" she exclaims in such genuine frustration that I almost want to believe her.

Instead, I shake my head in disgust.

Then I look down and see her slender hands form into fists. Could that be real frustration or continued acting on her part?

"What are you going to do to me?" she asks. "Am I Disqualified?"

But I don't reply and start to turn from her. *Let her squirm.*

"Wait!" she exclaims. "What is going to happen?"

I glance back at her. "You are going to be questioned continually until we have the information you are withholding."

"You mean, interrogated until I 'confess' to something?"

"Yes. You will remain here in custody until you do."

She begins shuddering again.

But I'm done with her. I start to go, except that something inside me causes me to pause, for some reason. And so, I turn again to look back at her, look her in those faultless blue eyes. "Tell me one thing at least," I say. "When you got me out of the shuttle chair, how did you release me from the flight harness?"

"What?" She frowns. "The what? Oh—there was a weird button. I squeezed it together, and it collapsed the harness."

I crane my neck slightly, and my wintry gaze stills on her. For a few heartbeats I contemplate Gwen Lark with her intimate eyes and clever words. "Thank you—for telling me at least one honest thing."

And then I leave her alone in the sterile chamber.

I ORDER her returned to the correctional cell to wait for more punitive action. My mind races and I begin to collect information on her and look through other evidence. Hours pass and I allow her older brother to see her briefly.

Intending to be impeccably *fair* as I build the case against her, I consult with her Instructors, four of whom are my own *daimon* officers. After a heated discussion with Nefir, Xelio, Oalla, Keruvat, and Instructor Warrenson, the consensus is, that in order to have a complete set of evidence, Gwen Lark must be given the opportunity to demonstrate her outrageous claim.

It's interesting to note that all the Instructors speak favorably of her even now; everyone is so willing to give her a chance to redeem herself. Xelio in particular tells me not to rush to conclusions, and Oalla thinks Lark is not capable of the high level of deception that I attribute to her.

Ker pulls me aside and says, "Go with your instinct, Kass, not your anger. I get it, we're all broken by what happened to Tiliar and the others. Seems that you're a little too emotionally invested in condemning her. Let's reexamine the facts and let her show us what she can do."

I continue to be highly doubtful of her vocal abilities. Indeed, my anger kindles at the mere thought of this nonsense being perpetuated. However, this is all a part of allowing the system of justice to do its job, so I relent and agree to the demonstration. We will let her prove that she can use voice commands well enough to bring down a falling orichalcum object the size of a shuttle. And when she fails (as she must), there will be no doubt or regret when I order her deserved *punishment*.

It is almost evening when we go to the airfield, prep a shuttle, and Gwen Lark is escorted before us to demonstrate her dubious vocal skills. A crowd of other Candidates has gathered to watch.

Gwen stands in the empty expanse, her messy brown hair getting tangled in the wind, while the sunset shines on her anxious face.

She seems so pure, so frail, so innocent....

No, this needs to stop.

I steel myself against the constant gnawing presence of doubt when it comes to her, and speak in my coldest Logos voice.

"Candidate Gwen Lark, today you made a claim that you were able to safely levitate and then land a shuttle just like this one, purely with your voice—a voice that is mechanically unassisted."

I look into her eyes as I speak, and my expression is neutral and impassive, veiled in so many layers that it's impossible to fathom. "I do *not* for a moment believe that you have this exceedingly rare ability. However, before further measures are taken against you, I have been advised to allow you to prove yourself one way or another."

She listens to me and I see the dawning comprehension in her eyes. Is terror also present there? Ah, now the moment of truth and judgment is at hand. She is faced with her own lies and has *dug her own hole*—to use a Gebi turn of phrase.

What will she do?

First, she stalls. While the overly lenient Instructor Warrenson offers her voice command tips and tries to be helpful (he's Gebi, and his sympathies are understandable), she claims her throat is parched and asks for water . . . so that she can sing.

I humor her, since this request makes sense, considering that she hasn't had any food or drink all day. One of her friends (the same stoic girl who had the foot injury) gives her a water bottle.

Gwen Lark takes the bottle, drinks, and I watch the water spill past her lips and run down her chin.

She then opens her mouth and out comes . . . *wonder*.

She leads with a Middle F tonic note to voice-key the shuttle, then does a rising octave slide, and the shuttle rises up into the blazing sunset sky.

Her voice, oh, her voice. . . .

It is Logos.

A shiver of awe—of something deep and primeval takes me even as I listen to her dark, deep mezzo soprano and watch the shuttle approach the clouds, then come back down again with perfect skill. The crowd screams and applauds, acknowledging her triumph.

And Gwen Lark—she turns to me in the very end and gives me a proud, insolent look full of righteous disdain.

I meet her eyes, and in that one moment I am *destroyed*.

Vanquished, slain.

Ruined and enchanted and devastated . . . by an Earth girl with true eyes and the impossible voice of Atlantis.

She has the authentic voice of the ancients, the heritage almost exclusively belonging to the divine Kassiopei Dynasty. A voice so rare that it has been extinct almost everywhere else on Atlantis, and undoubtedly on Earth.

How do we know? We don't, not for a fact. But, from all our advance reconnaissance observation of this planet and research about the state of modern Earth humanity, we have no evidence of it. We know that the Gebi have no orichalcum and hence no means of using or even knowing if they have the voice of creation. The very concept of the Logos voice, *logos anima mundi,* barely exists here in their collective memory, having died out together with our exodus over twelve thousand Earth years ago.

And yet, here she is. . . . Is it possible that she's not unique? That there might be others on Earth like her? Regardless, it's too late to do much of anything about it, at least within the parameters of our Earth Mission. The asteroid strike will obliterate those who remain, and those who Qualify for rescue (and who are therefore more likely to have better vocal abilities than the general population)—those we can (and will) test later.

Right now, everyone is congratulating Lark, telling her how remarkable her demonstration was. Nefir launches on his typical exalted explanation of Logos and its use in ancient history, while Oalla, Ker, and the others discuss and wonder about the implications.

All this while, the girl with the voice of a lark—so appropriately named, after an Earth songbird—the girl keeps glancing at me, probably to gauge my reaction.

In this moment, she is triumphant. I can sense her emotional arousal by the charge of energy that's almost palpable as it emanates from her. What pleasure she must derive from proving *me* wrong. . . .

This is *personal.*

I stand off to the side—away from the cluster of others as they surround her—and I stare into the distance in order to avoid having to look at her.

My mind is trying to take in, is processing this new reality of her stunning voice and all the implications. In one moment, she has gone from almost assuredly a terrorist, suspected murderer, and prisoner to a precious commodity.

She might still be all those other things. But she is also a naturally talented vocalist. And my Imperial Father will be very interested to hear of this. If not I, then Nefir will make certain that he is informed immediately.

YES, in those initial days it did not yet matter to me what might happen to her under such circumstances, with her completely at my Father's mercy . . . or at least I didn't allow myself to think that far.

AND SO, I gather myself the best I can and move toward Gwen Lark. My face must still reflect some vestiges of a strange expression, betraying me to her, before I'm able to hide my vulnerability.

"Candidate Lark," I say, as frankly as I can, while facing her. "This changes everything."

"Command Pilot Kass—how so?" She stares back at me—still half-insolent in the way she dares to address me, almost a parody of my own earlier taunts of her. And yet, she seems genuinely curious in asking. "What will you do now? What happens to me?"

"Because of your voice, its intrinsic value to us, we cannot simply set you aside. Therefore, we cannot Disqualify you or proceed with the normal course of legal actions," I say coldly, with some regret at having to now keep my anger in check. "However, don't think for a moment that you are relieved of suspicion of wrongdoing. The investigation into your role in the tragic sabotage will continue. But for the moment, you are no longer in custody."

"What? You're letting me go?" she says, amazed.

Curiously, she did not see that coming. *Bashtooh,* her eyes. . . .

Just like that, I feel an instant of softening. I stifle it without mercy.

"You may return to your Dorm and your classes. You will continue in the Qualification process, but you will be watched closely." I pause, and my lips form a severe line, as I focus on her.

I attempt to pierce her with my look, to see *through her* and learn the truth, all of it. If I have to, I will drown her with the pressure of my Imperial gaze in order to force the truth from her.

No more lies. . . .

"In addition," I continue, having made a certain personal decision, "it gives me no pleasure, but you will be working with me from now on. We will work on your voice. I will also train you in other things you will need to know, to improve your chances for Qualification."

"So . . . what does that mean?" Her expression is again full of anxiety, which I am beginning to take at face value.

"It means, I will see you in my office at eight, starting today. You know where it is. Now, dismissed."

And speaking curtly, I turn my back on her.

But oh, my spirit and soul, all of my thoughts, my very being stays behind, connected to her on a level I still don't understand.

WEEKS LATER, after our daily voice lessons and other regular interactions (highly controlled, one-on-one in my office), I've gotten to know even more of Gwen Lark—and myself.

I've come to see a sterling, authentic side of her personality that is clean, *real*, even though I still do not permit myself to fully acknowledge it.

I've discovered, she is ridiculous and curious. She makes me laugh in secret at her blundering insistence to keep trying in the face of failure (and pushing relentlessly when she thinks she's right). Her endearing oddity evokes uncalled-for pangs of amusement, even stupid tenderness in me, bringing out that vulnerable part of me that's normally hidden deep. Keruvat's advice returns to me periodically, "go with your instinct, not your anger."

I decide that my instinct is not reliable when it comes to her. Because my instinct is revealing a weakness inside *me*.

The day of Qualification Semi-Finals looms, and I send her off to an almost certain death and failure, knowing she's barely ready for the physical aspects of the ordeals and challenges that constitute these bitter trials. Even after all these weeks of training, she is sub-par in physical fitness, mediocre in Er-Du Combat and Quadrant weapons use. She's got skinny arms and pitiful, bony elbows. The only thing she has in her favor is her incredible voice.

I harden myself for her loss even as she leaves my office for the last time. And then on the morning of Semi-Finals I watch silently from my observation station the activities in the Arena Commons as the entire RQC-3 lines up—the frenzied media coverage, the races around the track, the choices of urban "game zones" that all Candidates make.

Lark chooses Los Angeles.

Which means that I have to follow her there. I cannot do anything to interfere or to assist her, but I can be there in the end, if she makes it past the hurdles and all the way up to the shuttles hovering over the city center.

I admit, that day of chaos is seared into my memory. . . . I spread my time thinly between my command duties of remotely supervising, delegating, and overseeing various aspects of the Semi-Finals at various locations and keeping an eye on *her* as she traverses the urban landscape.

Those of us in Atlantean High Command, which includes the Mission Fleet Commander and the three Command Pilots and our subordinate staff, have divided the immense task of overseeing major global "game zone" sites between us. I take responsibility for all five locations around the United States of America, plus quite a few additional international sites. In the course of the day, I fly back and forth around the planet when needed, and then I finish the day in Los Angeles.

I have her ID tracker programmed into a private batch of nano-cams that I launch remotely at the beginning of the event. The small cam pod rides with her in the shuttle on the way to California, and I instruct the Pilots to release the cams once they land, without giving them any more details. Again, I must remain neutral, no favoritism, no interference on anyone's behalf.

But . . . I can watch. And I do, with a pounding heart and knives ripping my gut, as she is almost killed multiple times and seriously wounded in her arm. The nano-cams follow her —together with a billion other nano-cams assigned to the event in this city, following every other Candidate.

She barely makes it. In the end, she and her younger sister both cling to the heat-enabled orichalcum batons, rising toward one of the last remaining transport shuttles. I make certain to transfer to that same exact shuttle during the last minutes of the competition. And I watch in abysmal despair as Gwen burns her hand, holding on to the fiery baton—holding on to the very end, because her little sister is clinging to *her* in turn, for dear life. . . .

If there are any prayers to any universal forces or deities to be said, I breathe them all in those last heartbeats, whispering pleas without moving the controlled line of my lips (all the while screaming in my mind on her behalf.)

Do not let go.

I wait at the doorway of the shuttle, watching Gwen and her sister embraced in a tumble of limbs, approach within a few feet, then within touching distance.

She sees me, as I lean into the wind, ready to intercept her.

I stand before them at the opening of the shuttle. As they levitate within reach, I put out my bare hand and place it directly upon the incandescent white middle of her baton.

It burns, oh, it burns! White agony fills me, and at once, death memories strike—of burning at the Rim of Ae-Leiterra—but none of it matters. *Burning, burning . . . endless white fury of the accretion disk. . . .*

Outwardly I never flinch as I make contact with the fire, becoming one with it, like an old friend, until in a matter of heartbeats it stops hurting (the nerve endings on my palm and fingers are destroyed). . . . I simply pull them both inward into the soothing darkness of the shuttle interior.

"You can let go now," I say softly, staring directly into her eyes.

Gwen does as I say, and starts to collapse, losing consciousness. I quickly discard the baton (it forcefully strikes the floor of the shuttle and continues to roll, still incandescent, to be dealt with later), ignore my ruined hand for the moment, and break her fall by grasping her with my one good hand and wrapping my arm around her.

Her sister staggers momentarily, establishing her footing, then moves in to support her from the other side.

Existing in the moment, personal pain and injury are

irrelevant to my body; I make arrangements to get Gwen Lark urgent, high-end medical treatment. There are other Candidates on the shuttle, many of them also injured, and I try my best not to show favoritism—everyone on board will get the same high-end care once we arrive. And as we begin to fly to the National Qualification Center campus, I allow myself to feel the incredible psychological relief of *knowing* that she's hurt but *alive*.

She made it this far, survived the Semi-Finals.

And so have I.

WHEN WE ARRIVE at the NQC in Colorado, I make sure all the Candidates on my shuttle receive the best treatment available (but my true attention is only on one of them). Gwen's hand is regenerated from its fourth degree burn that exposed her finger bones, and her gunshot wound healed. Only then do I bother to have the med techs work on my own hand with its milder third degree burn on the palm.

Still unconscious and well medicated, Gwen is taken to a hospital room to recuperate. The immense hospital is busy handling the influx of thousands of injured Candidates from all over.

I let her rest, while I return to my other numerous duties. The logistics of this NQC alone are immense, and my staff and Aides are hard at work.

However, first thing the next morning, allowing myself the gift of brief weakness, I visit her room.

For a few daydreams I observe her sleeping face, relaxed and innocent in the darkened room, with only the dawning light from the window to cast her in soft grey shadows. Her sister Grace appears to be asleep in the chair next to Gwen's bed, and I say nothing to disturb her. Eventually I leave, as quietly as I came in.

~

DAYS PASS, and the NQC in the United States is now my main base of operations. I commute daily from ICS-2 down to the planet surface, spending very little time on Earth while the Candidates train for the Finals. Only an Earth month remains, and then it will all be over.

I keep my focus on the tasks at hand, but often my thoughts slither past my guarded control and I *imagine* her, at any odd hours of day or night.

At one point an incident happens, directly related to the shuttle tampering investigation, and this time the correct Lark culprit is arrested. Little *hoohvak* Grace Lark is detained for being the one who obtained the stolen shuttle navigation chip and placed it in Laronda Aimes's jacket, framing her, regardless of her actual intent. This exonerates Gwen, but her sister must face the consequences—Disqualification. I feel a twinge of pity for her, even knowing the extent of her involvement.

Nefir contacts me in advance to let me know that the "big sister" is distraught, and begging an audience with me. I also find out that Gwen Lark has been going to various office buildings, harassing the guards and compound staff and *demanding* to see me—naturally. I would expect nothing less of her.

When I receive the text message from Nefir, I am at the CCO, seated at my desk and speaking via interstellar comms (which is why his surface-to-orbit message comes through immediately instead of being queued for morning when we open the firewall-secured relays). My interstellar personal call is with Lady Tirinea Fuorai, which is a rather delicate matter on any given day.

Ah, Lady Tiri, the lovely and tantalizing and terrible bane of my existence. . . .

She's the daughter of wealthy Lord Fuorai, and is my Father's choice of intended Bride and Consort for me. She is beautiful and horrible and unavoidable.

My Father expects me to select and formally name a Bride as soon as we return to Atlantis, and has made it clear that I must pick *her*—if I want to avoid his increased displeasure and an annual Rite of Sacrifice for the rest of my life.

To be honest, sometimes, in my most irritable moments, I weigh the pros and cons of either fate. What's truly worse? Anonymous procreative rituals with unknown invisible noblewomen, just once or twice a year? Or having to live with and *varqood* this spoiled and scheming High Court brat with her perfect physical attributes, fake smiles, and heartless, joyless, artifice—just so that she would bear me genetically ideal children to continue the Dynasty, while my Father enriches himself from the Fuorai holdings and influence?

I try to console myself that when I *varqood* her it would give me a good release, as long as I don't permit my emotions to get in the way. I'm definitely affected physically when she flaunts her body at me (again, I curse my "healthy" Kassiopei lust, so easily provoked and appeased, requiring constant vigilance to keep under control). It's the daily act of living with her that terrifies. I suspect, with time I would either adapt and harden my soul, or it would make me dead inside.

In short, Lady Tiri is a complicated and conflicted issue for me. I try to be open to her, even affectionate—such as in this very moment—but Nefir's message (showing up as a notification on the bottom of the screen) reminds me of Candidate Lark. And at once I feel the dissonance taking an upper hand, ruining the mood.

" . . . and they will all be there, and of course I have no choice but to invite them," Lady Tiri is saying in her permanently condescending tone when it comes to others. "You know I must invite them, because it is a *dea* meal reception on behalf of Lady Hathora, and so the dear old things have to accompany her, especially Dame Quaratha—who is not only rather slow these days, but has never been the sharpest wit *ever*—and I must say, her daft stories are worthy of at least two decades before any of us were born—"

Lady Tiri makes a tittering noise that is intended to be a very feminine giggle, and moves closer to the video display screen. Her airy, golden veil-scarf slips down artfully so that all I can see are smooth, exposed shoulders and the tops of her perfectly rounded *sohuru*, making her appear naked.

Naturally, my gaze lingers on her fine attributes. Then I reply in a polite, bland voice, "Why must you invite them if it's so tedious?"

"Ah, My Imperial Lord, you make me laugh! So charming of you to forget—but understandable, of course, with your important Fleet preoccupations," Tiri says with a flirtatious narrowing of her beautiful, completely opaque, green-gold-hazel eyes—which annoys me to no end. "You must recall that Dame Quaratha is related to Lady Hathora's second cousin's brother-in-law. . . ."

I raise one brow in weariness, but say nothing. Normally, I would make more of an effort, but after a long Fleet workday, I find *Atlantida* Court Protocol exhausting.

Lady Tiri cleverly notices that my interest in this topic is waning. And so . . . instead, she starts to inquire about *me*. "You mustn't overwork and tire yourself, My Imperial Lord," she says in a lilting, soothing voice that almost makes me believe her concern for me is genuine.

"Thank you, I'm fine," I reply, and give her a light smile.

At this point Lady Tiri pouts at me, so that I cannot help but observe her glossy, full lips. "I do so hate to disagree with My Imperial Lord in any way, but I believe you require more rest than you permit yourself. It comes with your lofty abilities, your admirable, truly *remarkable* energy. And yet—it's so ghastly, all your Fleet duties on behalf of these Gebi who are not half as grateful or appreciative of your Imperial efforts as they ought to be."

"No need to worry on my behalf, my Lady," I say. "But the Gebi are doing the best they can under very difficult circumstances. Imagine the Games of the Atlantis Grail—their Qualification incorporates many similar elements—"

"Ugh, no, I don't want to imagine anything of the sort," Tiri retorts with a tiny, pretty grimace. "So dreary and distasteful."

"Well, then," I conclude, without any more "distasteful" detail. "Overall, we're managing just fine, and eventually, we will be home."

"Oh, but that's months from now! A year, a tedious Gebi year, or maybe more! I can't wait to see you!" she exclaims, widening her eyes and looking at me with a perfectly executed expression of *intimate* welcome. "I can only envision how weary you are of being surrounded by drab Fleet uniforms and coarse, inconsequential speech. . . . Commoners are well and good in their own place, but to be exposed to them on a daily basis— oh, I have no words, My Imperial Lord, none sufficient, but to give you my most affectionate sympathies on your ordeal."

"I—appreciate your sympathies," I reply in a neutral manner.

Ah, the art of saying something inoffensive instead of speaking one's mind....

"How you must miss the dear, familiar splendor of your Imperial Father's Court, the magnificence of Poseidon, our fair City!" she continues. "Their barbaric customs, terrible Earth food—oh, I shall *cry* on your behalf, my dear, *dear*—Imperial Lord—"

"I beg you not to waste your tears on me, my *dear* Lady Tiri," I say with a thin, sarcastic smile, thinking, *Bashtooh*, if she cries....

"Oh, but I must!" Tiri interrupts, putting her hand over her mouth delicately. "How must you suffer!"

In the name of all that's holy, please don't put me through this, Tiri.

Fortunately, there are no tears, and instead she changes the subject mercurially. "I must say, I had the utmost pleasure of seeing the dearest Imperial Princess Manala—just the other day, in the Imperial Gardens. What a treasure she is, such delicate beauty, such charm of demeanor! I do wish your delightful sister was more comfortable expressing her tender feelings in my company, since she and I are such good friends already—and I have every hope of our *connection* becoming even *more*, once My Imperial Lord returns home—"

As usual, at least once during our conversations, Lady Tiri makes a hint about a "connection." In this case, Manala, my poor, innocent sister, is being used for this.

I ignore the hint and patiently continue to listen.

When I'm done communicating with Tiri (and listening to more of her vacuous Court gossip interspersed with blatant and annoying flattery toward me), I sit back and make the inevitable decision to see Gwen Lark tomorrow.

I TAKE my shuttle down the next morning and Lark is waiting for me at the airfield. We go into my office, and her emotional onslaught begins.

Gwen Lark seems to know exactly what to say to get to my sympathies, even if I don't show it and harden myself against her. She begs me to give her sister another chance, and throws every argument at me.

"I am sorry," I say in a controlled voice. "There is nothing that can be done. She is Disqualified and she is returning home."

"No," Gwen retorts, wild-eyed, and her voice rises in strength. *"I do not accept that."*

As she speaks, I can feel a tangible prickling sensation rising along the surface of my skin. The acoustics of it cause a ripple in the air and a reverb in the walls. So much power.

No, it cannot be. . . .

I frown, shake my head, while my gaze remains fixed upon her. It feels as if her voice has scraped me physically, that I must shake off an invisible touch.

"Candidate Lark, what did you just do?" I say, feeling easy anger awakening.

She frowns in turn. "I—what?"

"You just used a *compelling* power voice on me?" I say, in amazement and rising anger.

"I don't know what you mean!"

"Oh, I think you do."

I narrow my eyes, and my expression closes off completely.

"This has gone far enough. We're done." I get up from my chair and stand before her, pointing to the door.

That's when she begins to tremble. . . . Her breathing becomes shallow, and then she starts weeping in great, big, shuddering sobs.

Bashtooh! I can't even—what is she doing to me?

At the sight of her sobbing, I blink. In that moment I'm almost certain she can see a crack in my armor, glimpse the vulnerability in my eyes.

"I am truly sorry," I say quietly.

She continues choking on her tears, and raises her hands to wipe her face with her sleeves.

This is it . . . this is the moment to be *real*.

"There is also something else," I say in a carefully neutral voice. "Because of this unfortunate incident with your sister coming to light, you are now formally cleared of all charges. . . . There are no more suspicions regarding your actions in this. Therefore, I owe you an apology."

Varqood it, this was one of the most difficult things to say.

She stops crying. And suddenly she looks up. Her expression is blazing with energy. "No," she says. "You owe me a *life*."

Rawah bashtooh!

I blink again. And then I take a step toward her.

"That is true . . ." I say softly, while my mind is spinning with so much, so *much*. . . .

"I saved you from that burning shuttle," she utters in a wooden voice drained of all emotion. She appears driven only by a single focus.

"Yes. . . ."

"So you *owe* me!" she cries in a resonant voice of power. "A life for a life! Give me my sister's life!"

I've been holding my breath without realizing it, and suddenly I exhale—even as I make my decision. My heart lurches painfully as I think of my own sister Manala and what I would do for her....

Gwen Lark stares up at me with her fierce, remarkable eyes, breathing fast, waiting.

There is a long pause....

"Okay," I say at last. And then I return to my desk. I push forward one of the mech arms that extends the command console and monitor, lowering it over my desk surface. And I begin the process of reinstating the little sister. Since the ACA has Disqualified her and removed her Candidacy—the entirety of her ID data and all her current points—I cannot reverse the decision, not even with my level of authority, but I can reinstate her ID. Grace Lark will be given a new blank ID token and will have to begin points accumulation from scratch.

I explain all of this to Gwen, who immediately offers up her own points to her sister. Just as immediately I refuse. I will not have her throw her own life away in exchange for her sister's.

I couldn't bear it if she did....

"But what if I *choose* to do that, for her?" Gwen exclaims, her eyes once more brimming with despair.

"I do not permit it," I say coldly, with perfect control. "We need you and your voice—on behalf of Atlantis."

"But it is *my* choice!"

"Not entirely—not if your choice affects far more than you or your sister."

She stares at me, stunned.

I continue to watch her with my unreadable Imperial mask.

"But—" she says, as her outrage starts to build. "I don't understand! How can you tell me what I can or cannot do with my own life? Don't you have a *heart*? What about basic human compassion? Have you no clue what it's like to stand by and not help your own family—the people you most care about—when you absolutely have the means to do it?"

As she speaks, I freeze, holding myself utterly still. A world of agony, of past memories, of all my life, fills my head with a ringing clamor. *If only she knew . . . if only.*

No.

Her eyes, their wounded terrible judgment—it is *destroying* me yet again. But she will never know.

"Are you finished?" I say after a terrible pause. My voice has grown low and very soft, like the slither of an Imperial serpent. Under such circumstances, I've been told I am terrifying.

But Gwen Lark doesn't know when to stop. Moving stiffly, awkwardly, she nears my desk, and leans forward, almost against her own will, exclaiming, then babbling, "Please! I'll do anything you want me to do! *Anything!* Just let me help her! Look, I am begging you! Anything you want! Take it! Tell me if there's anything I can do, anything I have that I can give you. . . ?"

What is she saying? Does she even realize? Or is it intentional? A strange frisson of sensation passes through me, a light electric shock.

The implications of what it is she's saying, what it is she is offering me in her desperation. . . . Bashtooh, *am I misreading her? Because it seems my body understands only too well.*

Before my body starts to respond, I slam all the force of my trained will over my rampant thoughts and imagination. *She mustn't know.*

We face each other at close proximity, our gazes locked in intensity.

"You have *nothing*," I say suddenly, imbuing my words with controlled derision. "There is nothing you have that I want."

Again, she appears stunned. "What about my Logos voice?"

"Your voice has value for Atlantis, which is already a given. If you Qualify, we have you." I pause, and choose my words very carefully, maintaining the same fine sub-current of disdain. "I thought you were offering something for *me*."

By all gods—I've said it....

At once, her face turns red. "I—" Her words trail off. There's an unbearable long pause.

"Look," I finally break the silence, and my tone softens. "You got what you wanted, Lark. I reinstated your sister, and she has a fair chance of earning back most if not all of her points. Under the circumstances, it is absolutely *the best* I can do for her—or for you. In fact, I think you should be grateful right now. What do you say?"

In that moment I truly pity her. Gwen Lark appears suddenly worn out, emotionally depleted, her normally lively features slackened. Resignation and despair quench the bright energy and the *clarity* in her eyes. It's as if she realized at last that she can do nothing more; has nothing to offer, nothing to barter with....

I'm right, and somehow, I'm deeply sorry to be.

"Thank you," she says to me quietly.

I nod. "I am glad this is resolved. In the next hour your sister will be discharged, and her belongings returned to her Dorm."

"For real?" A spark of hope rekindles her demeanor.

"Yes." I feel relief also, followed by a moment of amusement. "Now I strongly recommend you get back to your own Dorm and schedule. Strange as it may seem, I have other things to deal with than Lark family drama."

She nods, then mutters something barely intelligible that sounds like "Okay."

I watch as she turns around and heads for the door. Just before she exits, I say, "Before you go—we need to continue your regular voice training. Be here tomorrow night at eight."

Startled, she glances again at me. "But—I thought you have other things to do?"

"Lark," I say. "Just be here at eight."

And the next stage of our interactions begins.

AT THE NQC the training days and weeks pass by quickly, and I am immersed in work, as the weather starts warming up here in the Eastern Plains of Colorado. I continue to see Gwen Lark regularly for her evening voice lessons, and it's getting harder and harder for me not to admit that my time with her is not merely a necessary duty and the nurturing of her Logos voice, but a secret personal pleasure.

I find that I look forward to 8:00 PM every night with a strange obsessive relief, knowing that I will finally *have her to myself*, here in the small office room.

What does that even mean? During the day she is out there, training, interacting with her fellow Candidates many of which have become friendly, her Instructors, her siblings, even random NQC staff. I have no claim on even a moment of her time or her attention.

And why should I? What in the world is happening to me, that I find myself viscerally aware of the fact that somewhere on this large campus, Gwen Lark is moving about and living her life?

There's another thing.

Candidate Logan Sangre is definitely more than a friend to her. Early on, I checked into his background, and discovered that he comes from her home location, and was a student in her high school, so they knew each other even before. Furthermore, from what I've observed, Gwen is romantically interested in him.

According to the NQC and RQC rules of conduct, they may not be "dating" in public but I realize that human nature will reassert itself. We cannot fully control Candidates' intimate behavior, not even with all our security measures and observation cameras in place. Our stern warning to them is more of a threat, and unless the misbehavior is blatant, it cannot be enforced.

I try not to think too far in that direction. But sometimes I cannot help but check camera footage . . . and I discover stolen kisses and touches between Candidate Lark and Candidate Sangre.

The first time I stumble upon it, it feels like the wind has been knocked out of me. A cold, unbearable sensation floods me, rising from the pit of my stomach. I pause the security video feed and close the viewer program. And I stare before me at the blank monitor screen, even as my blood rings in my temples.

And then I stop looking altogether, afraid to see any footage of her, because an urgent distress rises inside me at the very thought of what I might find, and I know very well that I may *not* think that way. It is not for me to think that way about any Candidate.

About *her*.

It's none of my concern whom Candidate Lark kisses or has a relationship with. And yet. . . .

How far along are they? Does he varqood *her?*

Enough, stop.

I stop the onrush of madness that sweeps through me like a

tornado every time I imagine certain things, and I focus on my work.

One incident sits strangely with me. It happens on the day after our confrontation in regard to reinstating her sister.

We have voice training, during which strange tensions rise in regard to what happened earlier when Lark pled with me about her sister and inadvertently used a *compelling* voice on me. Lark begins with an apology, but as usual in our conversation, things get off on a tangent. I explain to her that the *compelling* voice is not only immoral but illegal. At which point Lark babbles some awkwardly confrontational things— almost insults—and, come to think of it, I tell her some hostile things also.

The inexplicable energy charge rings in the air between us. . . .

In the course of our exchange, she calls me "uptight" and tells me to "just chill, take a break, already." I tell her to get out of my office (it's the end of class) and then she practically runs from me.

I decide I'm so overheated that I need a break indeed, and so I head to the large training pool for an evening swim, meeting up with a few of my *astra daimon* officers.

Keruvat, Oalla, and I swim laps, trying to ignore the noisy crowds of Candidates frolicking in the cool water.

And then I notice Gwen Lark. She's there, splashing around with her friends and one of them is Logan. At that point I put up walls of psychological distance. I force myself *never* to look in their direction, not even once.

After we're done swimming, we get out of the pool. On the way to the lockers to retrieve our clothing, we have to walk the length of the immense pool, and unavoidably pass by the spot with Gwen and her friends.

I walk along the side of the pool, dripping water, my hair plastered to my scalp, mildly self-conscious of the fact that I'm soaking wet, and wearing nothing but swimming shorts—not that it had ever occurred to me before to be self-conscious of my own appearance. What kind of *bashtooh* new anxiety is this? Good thing I don't show it, keeping my back straight. All they get to see is my confident outward demeanor of a commanding officer.

I make a point of not "noticing" Gwen Lark. Instead, I observe the panorama of all the Candidates in the water.

With my peripheral vision I see one of Gwen's female friends teasingly punch the other, as I approach, and hear them giggling when one of them says "Stop drooling!"

With a twinge of amusement, I realize they're referring to me.

And then I hear Gwen speak—at the exact moment that I move past.

"You know," she says in an elevated voice, so that it carries (almost intentionally) to me. "What is it with Atlanteans and *eyeliner?* They must use waterproof or permanent eye makeup that it doesn't get smudged in the water, even after all that swimming. Talk about vanity!"

Suddenly I feel a strange cold come over me, despite the heat of the evening. All traces of amusement dissipate, and I am feeling bizarre, inexplicable . . . *anguish.*

"Good point," one of Gwen's friends replies.

"And what's up with all that ridiculous metallic hair dye?" Lark continues loudly. "So okay, it doesn't run in the water. But really, eventually it would—wouldn't you think?"

They know nothing. Not their fault they have certain assumptions about me—about all of us.

"I bet they probably need to re-apply touch-ups every time

they wash their hair," another girl says. "That kind of metallic hue must be really difficult to make permanent."

At this point, I steel myself and keep walking away stiffly, not looking to my side, trying not to listen to these Gebi anymore.

She thinks it's vanity. . . . The Kassiopei gold hair, the genetic tracings on the eyelids of my wedjat *eyes.*

No, stop.

Not her fault.

I continue walking, putting distance between us. I know Oalla is right behind me, so I don't want to give her any reason to notice *anything.*

Not that there's anything to notice.

I am not sure. . . .

I keep moving in the direction of the lockers.

HERE AND NOW, on board ICS-2, on the way to Atlantis, I'm interrupted from my thoughts by a knock on my cabin door. It is getting late, close to midnight according to the ship's Earth-time simulator clock, and I can't imagine who it could be. Possibly Ker or Xel, coming by to see if I'm up for a night jog around the ship on the Observation Deck. If there was an emergency, the third-shift crew on duty would call me instead. For that matter, so would the *daimon*, who would message me instead of dropping in unannounced. They have to keep up at least some semblance of Fleet command structure and commanding officer decorum.

I stand up and go to open the door. It's Consul Suval Denu.

"Consul," I say, mildly surprised to see him. "Is there something the matter? May I be of assistance with anything?"

Consul Denu—attired in a somewhat more casual gilded robe for the evening, and wearing a less lofty wig—gives me his perfect courtly bow, and offers profuse apologies for disturbing "My Imperial Lord" so late.

"With your gracious permission, My Imperial Lord, I would like a bit of advice," he says to me finally, gesturing with his hand for me to step outside. "Will you grace me with your presence for a brief stroll before bedtime?"

"Of course," I say, closing the door behind me and follow him out into the ship corridor.

We walk rather slowly (I slow down for the sake of the Consul who likes to move at a leisurely pace, often wearing elevated platform shoes with wobbly heels for the sake of annoying Court fashion, even here on a Fleet vessel). Passing Command Deck sections, we head for the nearly empty Observation Deck, and at first, all I hear on the way are pleasantries and the usual snippets of conversations Suval Denu had with the ACA or with my Imperial Father. I know better than to interrupt him, and my ingrained Court manners take over.

Finally, Consul Denu touches my arm lightly and we pause before the grand view of the cosmos streaming outside the large floor-to-ceiling windows. "What vast and terrible beauty, out there," he says with a sweeping hand gesture. "Just to think of where we are right now is breathtaking."

"It is indeed," I reply politely. "But it is getting rather late, and is there something you wanted to discuss with me, Consul?"

"Ah, my dear, yes," the Consul says hurriedly, patting me on the arm then adjusting the silk of his wide sleeve. I note his impeccably polished nails and the glitter of gems on his rings. "What I wanted to ask is your *advice* on what I might convey to the Imperial Sovereign, Your Father, when I call him again tomorrow. This evening he had asked me about you—namely, your stance about certain matters of the heart. He strongly implied that he wants to know your position in regard to a certain young lady who would very much like to be even more to you than she already is."

"Who?" I ask. For some *hoohvak* reason my first thought jumps to Gwen Lark, even though I know it's ridiculous.

But Consul Denu continues in the convoluted mode of Courtly discourse. "As I said, My Imperial Lord," he replies, again sweeping his hand to point at the vast cosmic panorama in the window. "A terrible beauty! *Vastly* terrible!"

And suddenly I comprehend. He is referring to Lady Tiri, because once, months ago—just once, and it's remarkable he remembered my words—I spilled my mind in his presence, half joking, and commented that Tirinea Fuorai may be a beauty but she is a "terrible beauty."

"I see," I reply.

"Good," the Consul says with a light smile. "Such a delight for your humble servant to know that my modest words are understood. And so, what should I tell the Imperial Sovereign? And of course, My Imperial Lord is clear that whatever I impart is precisely what you would like me to say, not more not less."

In other words, the sly and diplomatic Consul, in his roundabout way, is saying that he will only pass on to my Father what I *want* him to know and not necessarily what is the actual reality.

I consider briefly what would be the most advantageous thing to say to my Father (using Consul Denu's clever lips), given our intense conversation earlier. And then—regardless of what the outcome of my upcoming decision will be tonight—I choose the most careful and safest reply.

"Tell my Father that, as far as *how* I'm doing, I am terribly overwhelmed with my mission duties and have very little time to waste on anything else. However, I am entirely satisfied to choose a Bride as soon as we land. He may rest assured it will happen immediately, and on that I give my oath as his Son and Imperial Crown Prince and Heir."

"Ah, splendid," the Consul says with a graceful inclination of his head, smiling gently at me. "I will be sure to relay this, knowing the reply will make the Imperial Sovereign extremely pleased."

I nod. "Then you have my *advice*. Is there anything else?"

Consul Denu chuckles. "Not unless there is something more for me to pass along on My Imperial Lord's behalf. I gently suggest that if there is, we leave it for another occasion. This is plenty."

I chuckle also. "My deepest appreciation, Consul. And now, if you don't mind walking back on your own—"

I don't even need to complete the thought.

Consul Suval Denu bows before me. "But of course, My Imperial Lord, you need a few more moments to experience the *terrible beauty* of the sights before us. This Observation Deck is a wonder. And you need a little more time to think."

Time to think. . . .

Somehow, I suspect the Consul knows about my Father's call to me this morning. He knows and suspects about Lark and my true conflicted stance. And he knows I'm still unsure, still making that difficult decision, tonight.

"*Nefero niktos*, Consul," I say. "Yes, I will stay here a little while longer."

"And I will leave My Imperial Lord to it and be on my way at once—may you have a splendid night!" And he heads back in the direction we came from, his gilded robe sailing behind him.

After the Consul is gone, I pause to linger at the nearest window and stare into the blackness of space, with nothing but the midnight silence and the gentle hum of the ship to keep me company.

And I think once again, sinking into memories. Ah, the memories this Observation Deck evokes....

I RECALL one day on this same Observation Deck many months ago. It's soon after Qualification, during the earliest days of our return journey on board the Fleet ark-ships, this time filled to capacity with the millions of Earth refugees and resources. On that day—with the Fleet still moving through Sol's system, and just having flown past Saturn—something happens that changes everything.

It must be noted that at this point, despite some stunning odds, Gwen Lark has Qualified and is officially working for me as an Aide at the CCO. Together with hundreds of other Earth Cadets and Civilians, and quite a few of the Fleet crew, she has gone to the Observation Deck to watch the passage of Saturn.

I decide to join them all, and take a detour to Observation directly from my staff meeting with various deck officers. This is completely spontaneous, unintentional. I don't even know if Lark would be there, nor am I thinking about her, for once....

By the time I get there, it's close to 10:00 PM, pseudo-Earth clock time, and the crowds on the Observation Deck have thinned out. All barracks and dorms adhere to the 10:00 PM lights out, so most Gebi have returned, in time for bed, after a very long first official day as Civilians and Cadets.

A few linger, gazing into the dark cosmic panorama outside the ship's array of floor-to-ceiling windows.

I stroll slowly, pausing at different sections of windows, taking in not only the view of space but the young humans on deck—all of them either under my command or my direct responsibility.

Everyone, precious cargo on my ship.

And then I notice *her*.

Gwen Lark stands exceedingly still, taking occasional shuddering breaths, and looks out into the void. Moments float away in silence.

Instinctively I pause my leisurely stroll a few steps away and also grow still. With my back against a dark portion of the wall between two windows, I stand frozen, mesmerized, looking at her.

The slender girl before me looks vulnerable and so terribly alone. As more and more of the other people leave, the more apparent it becomes that she is an island—motionless, solitary, silent.

I note her oddly graceful lines of neck and shoulders. At present, she is completely natural—not at all self-aware—and seems to have forgotten herself to the point of "forgetting" her usual awkwardness.

A strange, soft pity overcomes me.

I read her body language, her demeanor so clearly, for once. It occurs to me, how strange and isolated her personal situation is, compared to the others on board this ship. As an Aide to the CCO, unassigned to any standard shipboard group, she doesn't really have to be anywhere. She doesn't need to obey any barracks curfew.

At least during Qualification she was a Candidate like the others. But now, she's somewhere between being an Earth refugee and an Atlantean crew member.

Neither here nor there. An aimless nobody, out of place.

She doesn't belong.

What is she thinking now, watching the grand infinity through the windows, and her whole world recede?

I don't know how much time passes, as we both stand—she, staring out at the black cosmos outside, and I, staring at her. Possibly half an hour.

The illumination of the Observation Deck is soft and low, a kind of permanent twilight, with the floor plasma lights supplying just enough illumination to move around safely. This is mood lighting, to allow those who choose to be here to meditate upon the view of the universe.

At some point, no one else is here on this portion of the deck; everyone has left. Occasional Atlantean crew on duty pass the corridor, but that's it.

She stands alone, and desperately watches the receding Earth—it has become a faint star, a *dot* of blue. I image what it must be like for her, seeing all of her former life encapsulated in a dot, tiny, infinitesimal, precious, vulnerable, even now passing beyond sight. I'm reminded of my own first, heart wrenching moment of seeing blue-green Atlantis fall away, years ago when I took my first shuttle flight beyond orbit and into the outer reaches of Hel system space.

How well I understand, it is her last anchor, her one and only point of familiar connection, and in a few more moments, it will be doubtful if she's looking at anything at all.

Suddenly I hear her whisper, "Good-bye, little Pale Blue Dot."

She must know—the Earth has dissolved into the darkness, has been swallowed by the cosmic grandeur all around. Only Sol is outside the window, and it alone remains an anchor point of visual reference.

My heart lurches with a sympathetic response. Even the

simple sound of her voice after all that silence has a strange effect on me.

Suddenly she staggers, taking a few steps to right herself, and puts out her hand toward the nearest inner wall of the deck, away from the windows. Gwen Lark is shaking, and her face is streaming with tears. . . .

Up to this point I have been quiet and still as death, motionless and hardly breathing.

And yet suddenly, it seems she has become aware of my presence.

She knows that *someone* nearby is watching her from the shadows of the Observation Deck.

She panics, looks around.

She sees me, standing in the narrow dark place between two window panels, just off to the side.

Should I be guilty for impinging on her privacy? Yes, probably. But on the other hand, I was also taken by the moment. Once I had stopped to watch her it was inevitable that I remain. . . . Strangely enough, I was afraid to disturb or even frighten her by my presence, seeing her in this fragile state. And the more she lingered, the more awkward it became for me to make myself known or extricate myself from this intimacy.

I was not thinking ahead, merely being in the moment— exactly as she was.

And now, in the faint light, all she can likely distinguish is the fact that someone is there. She must be alarmed and anxious, and unsure how long a stranger has been watching her.

Just then, she takes a deep shuddering breath, probably thinking, how dare this stranger intrude upon her moment of privacy?

Guilt and regret come over me. *I didn't mean to impose.*

We act in tandem. She takes a step toward the windows, toward me, acknowledging my presence, while I separate from the shadows and come forward toward her.

She recognizes me.

"Oh!" she exclaims, showing immediate embarrassment, her stance, her very body becoming awkward—now that she knows for a fact she's not alone. "Command Pilot, I'm sorry I didn't see you," she mutters and hastily wipes her eyes, then exhales a resigned breath. Apparently, she understands that I've seen her being vulnerable all this time, and just maybe, it's *okay*.

Just then, she turns her glittering eyes up at me, meeting my gaze directly.

And in the silent, raw moment of low light, with the immensity of the universe flowing outside the windows, something strikes me about her....

Her eyes.

They are introspective, full of alien dreams, intimate, so very *blue*.

I realize in that split instant of cosmic connection that I have *seen* them before—seen their perfect clarity, their familiar rightness.

And I don't mean our daily interactions and routine.

I have seen her eyes when I was dying at Ae-Leiterra . . . surrounded by the forces of the black hole accretion disk. I saw them in that last swirl of living images—my memories of family and loved ones, a glimpse of Elikara's brown eyes, and then, these blue eyes of a stranger, pulled out of my impossible future.

Suddenly, time is blurring....

I stand, fixed in terrible, universe-upending wonder.

Her eyes were the last thing I saw in those final moments

before the wondrous rainbow cloud of the alien *pegasei* enveloped me, taking me into an *otherplace*, bypassing death.

How did I not realize this earlier? What kind of blind, *hoohvak* fool am I? Her eyes, her eyes, oh, her *eyes*!

My mind rings with grand awareness.

From that first moment on the first day when our gazes met at Pennsylvania RQC-3, when Gwen Lark asked me "Why Combat," the circle between us was completed—a closed circuit of looping time, confirming our intimate bond of entanglement.

I was pierced by her eyes and did not understand why.

All these months ago. . . . All these wasted moments of time, when my subconscious mind *knew* her, while my obtuse waking self did *not* (only obsessed and dreamed about her, against all reason and logic, despite suspicions and doubts).

Now I do.

Now, stricken by truth, I say nothing in reply to her—I'm unable to speak at all—only continue to stare. She must wonder, why am I silent? Not to mention, what am I doing here, hiding in the shadows?

Not getting a response from me, only this peculiar silence, she speaks again.

"It's really late, I know, I should be getting back . . ." she says awkwardly in a near whisper, her voice cracking from recent tears.

Somehow, I regain my ability to speak.

"Go . . . get some rest," I reply, and my quiet voice is gentle like never before.

But now it's her turn—Gwen Lark is staring at me, as though she too has just experienced a moment of preternatural recognition.

The oval of her face is softened even more in the twilight

illumination of the deck, so the focus is all on the eyes. . . .

"Okay . . ." she whispers, blinking away what is possibly a surge of feeling.

Even though my universe has been upended and my mind is still spinning, there is nothing more I can say or do now.

And so, I nod, reverting to my Fleet command role, then turn away from her and walk quickly in the direction of the interior of the ship.

IN THE HERE AND NOW, I retrace my steps of that memorable night almost a year ago, returning from the Observation Deck to my cabin.

My thoughts continue to shuffle all memories, forcing myself to admit my feelings, my obsession, my fascination with Gwen Lark.

She has gone from being merely interesting, to being the most interesting person in my world.

I get back to my cabin and pour myself a glass of chilled *qvaali* from a bottle I keep in the locked compartment near my bed together with my few private belongings. (A small sketch notebook. A few digital pens. A box of spare tiny *astroctadra* pins worn in secret by the *daimon*. A private encoded PCDU wrist communication unit programmed with a direct interstellar comm line to the Imperial Palace.)

My gaze returns to my black armband that I'd removed earlier, expecting to be going directly to bed, before Consul Denu interrupted my plans.

My gut wrenches painfully with the decision before me, still unmade.

I continue to sort through my memories.

ONCE I RECOGNIZE Gwen's eyes and accept my own emotional connection to her, the events of the months that follow unfold in an inevitable line of cause and effect.

In my mind our interactions subtly gain levels of intimacy, more and more each day, even though I can never be sure of her own inner state or feelings toward me. I might have leveled up when it comes to her, but she—she is still with Logan Sangre.

Until she's not.

There's a whole series of events, a chain of painful, terrifying, even bitterly awkward experiences.

There are two terrifying events in regard to Lark; hard to say which one takes precedence in my mind.

The first event is the hostage crisis with Terra Patria, masterminded by Earth Union, when I almost lose her to the terrorists—and probably reveal far too much of my feelings for her by the extent to which I go to protect her.

The second—and possibly the worst, because in this situation I literally have no control over the outcome, no means to come racing to her rescue—is what happens during the first Quantum Stream Race.

Gwen Lark and her Pilot Partner Hugo Moreno spin out and Breach outside the Boundary of the Quantum Stream and are lost in the great interstellar space for a short period of time during which I *lose* my mind.

Over and over, I check systems, run reports from various proximity sensors in the area along the race course where their shuttle was last seen. I ask subordinate officers for more location data. And all the meanwhile, as my hope dies, I too die a slow death, a thousand times, with each heartbeat. . . .

Finally, Fleet Pilot Instructor Mithrat Okoi contacts me with the news that the shuttle has been found—apparently it showed up again on the control display grid—and he's meeting them at the shuttle bay. With an impossible feeling of relief mixed with anger I tell him to send them both up to my office immediately.

When Lark and Moreno arrive at the CCO, panting for breath, I am pacing near my desk. My despair has turned to joyful fury at her.

She is alive! And now I'm ready to kill her myself....

The moment I see her I whirl around and stop.

I stare at her with the force of all my pent-up *being*—all my loss and despair incorporated into my gaze, barely keeping a mask over that ocean of furious intensity.

"Moreno and Lark! *Where have you been?*" The words burst out of me like hammer blows. I'm not using a power voice but I might as well be.

Both Lark and Moreno cringe at my onslaught.

She barely meets my gaze. "I am very sorry, Command Pilot," she says. "We were making our final turn in the Race when we Breached out of the Quantum Stream. And then we somehow got back in."

"You certainly did."

As I speak, I look at *her*—only her alone, ignoring her Pilot Partner completely.

A moment of silence.

"Your shuttle," I say, while my expression cannot contain the primal emotions that are pressing to explode. "It disappeared completely off the Fleet Grid. Missing for *forty-nine minutes*."

Forty-nine minutes of darkness and soul death, every heartbeat driving me closer to the black....

"Yes, that would be the time we were out there in interstellar space . . ." Hugo Moreno says carefully.

She nods to confirm—as if that would make a difference.

"And then," I continue, glancing at Moreno briefly but returning all my painful focus to her, "and then ICS-2 Shuttle #72 miraculously reappeared."

"Yes . . ." she says softly.

I frown. In the quiet of the office, my breathing is elevated as I hold myself in check . . . just barely.

Control the breathing, don't let her see your pitiful mess, your utter weakness. . . .

"Here's the thing," I say. "In the *exact* moment when shuttle #72 reappeared on the Grid, the global QS sensors registered a sharp irregular change in the frequency of the entire Quantum Stream. But that is not all—the new QS field frequency was the same as that of your incoming shuttle."

"So . . . what does that mean?" Moreno mutters.

"It means—" I pause, while my gaze bores into *her* and her alone, again ignoring Hugo Moreno. And then I say softly: "What happened was impossible—a fluke. Consider yourselves lucky to be alive."

They both stare at me in silence.

I tear myself away from them *(stop looking at her . . . stop, just stop. . . .)* and begin to pace.

"Cadet Moreno," I say. "You are dismissed. Return to your barracks. Your QS Race Score is 23 out of a possible 100, which puts both of you in the dismal #624 last place for this ship. Be glad you are alive."

"Thank you, Command Pilot," Moreno says densely, like the *hoohvak* that he is. "I am. . . ."

And he salutes me, gives Lark a fleeting, nervous glance, and exits the office.

Lark and I remain alone.

For a few seconds neither one of us says anything. And then I go to my desk and sit down. I lean back in my chair and put my hands behind my head.

"Sit down, Lark. We need to talk." My words are deceptively composed.

She approaches my desk stiffly and takes one of the visitor chairs. She sits motionless, and doesn't quite meet my eyes. I suspect that feelings inside her are also churning—joy, relief, terror. . . .

"All right, what really happened out there?" I say in a hard voice, watching her. "Tell me everything."

And she does. She speaks haltingly, and I suspect that she's not giving me the whole story. In the end she looks up at me with a strange, haunting look in her eyes.

My own expression in that moment is probably a mess, because what I feel is raw and terrifying. I lean forward, with my elbows resting on the desk. My clenched fist presses hard against the polished surface.

"What you did," I say. "It is not something that has ever been done by anyone who is not of Imperial Kassiopei blood."

She blinks. "Oh. . . . What did I do exactly?"

"You *keyed* the Quantum Stream to *yourself*." My gaze burns at her. "It had nothing to do with the shuttle you were piloting. It was all *you*. You did not merge back into the Quantum Stream by matching its natural frequency. You did something that *forced* the Quantum Stream to match its frequency to *yours*!"

"But—" Suddenly she appears breathless and faint. "How does that work? I thought you could only *key* orichalcum objects?"

I exhale, my energy levels softening. Right now, how I wish I could pour the truth of all things into her mind. . . .

"Orichalcum can be keyed because it has unusual

quantum-level properties," I say. "It happens to be uniquely unstable at the quantum level, permanently. Orichalcum is a transitional metal, always in quantum flux, and for that reason it can be manipulated in unusual ways."

I pause, thinking carefully of what else I may divulge, run my fingers slowly along the desk surface. "To acoustically levitate an object in regular 3D space, sound waves must bombard the object from three directions, surrounding it. Orichalcum, being in quantum flux, *entangles itself* with sound waves at a molecular level so that at any given moment its particles instead *surround* the sound. It 'wraps' itself against sound, creating the same effect. Instead of being surrounded by sound waves, it surrounds sound waves at the quantum level."

"That's wild," she whispers, her typical intellectual curiosity sparking in her eyes.

Oh, her eyes!

"The reason I tell you this is because you need to understand that quantum level manipulation lies at the heart of everything—all our technology." I never take my gaze off her; truly, I'm unable to . . . "What I've just told you is something no other Earth scientist, no Earth human being knows. And the reason I tell you this is because your abilities are amazing—even for an Atlantean."

She breathes very slowly, looking at me with so much expectation, so much *life* in her eyes. "Wow. Thanks—I guess?"

I continue watching her. Finally, I can no longer keep silent on the one thing, one *primal thing* I really want to say to her.

"I—" Raw and unfettered, my words come pouring out. "I didn't know what to *think* in that moment when you were *gone*. That moment when your shuttle dropped off the Fleet Grid, was—"

My words trail off. . . . Rather, I clamp them off with a force of will, like a tourniquet over a gushing wound.

There's silence.

She meets my eyes.

Suddenly, there's a universe of wordless communion between us.

When I speak at last, my voice is gruff with barely-checked emotions. "In short—I am very glad you made it back."

Ah, the understatement of the century.

"I'm glad too." She gives me a tiny smile.

The sweetness of it . . . the delicate curves of her lips. . . .

Immediately I frown, hardening my expression, slamming on my mask. "Now then, what happened today needs to remain a secret," I say in a cool manner. "There will be questions raised by the Commander, but we will not be disclosing details of the Quantum Stream anomaly to anyone else. The public will only know that you and Moreno managed to get back by normal means—you found the right frequency, matched it, keyed the shuttle to it, et cetera. In fact, do whatever it takes to convince your own Pilot Partner that's what happened, so that he also doesn't talk in a way to raise suspicions and questions."

"Okay." She nods. "What then should I do if people ask probing questions?"

I raise one brow. "You tell them whatever is in the Emergency Protocol. In the meantime, you and Moreno are officially in last place, and you get no special treatment, no 'extra credit' score for making it back alive out of the Breach."

She tightens her lips, starts to frown. "Doesn't bode well for my progress as a Pilot, does it?"

I snort, amusement brimming inside me—now that once again I know how to *feel*, know the meaning of *joy*. "No, it does not."

And then I meet her gaze once more "However—well done, Lark."

And I dismiss her.

~

AND THAT'S the most *terrifying* event when it comes to Gwen Lark, when she comes closest to being truly lost to me.

The most *awkward* happens during the Quantum Jump event, when we're thrown together by circumstances. She ends up here in my cabin on ICS-2, lying next to me in my own bed as the Fleet makes the Jump across the universe.

And then . . . my memories make me go up in flames. I remember daring to wrap myself around her in the narrow bunk, our proximity, holding her carefully, telling her to "breathe slowly" until the world goes dark. I remember waking up after the Jump happens, and then holding her again—this time as Jump Sickness manifests in her as anxiety and panic.

"It's okay . . ." I tell her in a thick voice, letting her struggle against the quantum effects. "Lie still. Try to lie still. Breathe slowly now—"

Even as she moans in frustration, I repeat, "It's okay, just breathe."

Until she starts tearing at herself, her own body, her hair; pulls at the security harness, the blanket underneath us, and her fingers tug at my shirt. She even grabs my hair, her fingers digging into my scalp (which I find strangely arousing; charges of electricity run through me at her touch).

"Hold on just a few minutes longer," I whisper. "It's okay."

Just then, her female undergarment that the Gebi call a bra, breaks in the back, and she is suddenly naked before me, with her two beautiful large breasts.

I lose my mind, and any vestiges of control over my own body.

My Kassiopei lust roars to life, awakening the serpent below. In moments, my *varqooi* is hard, and my hands are all over her body. I squeeze her and she moves against me almost as if she too is aroused (something I may not think about, no). A few heartbeats of hoarse breathing, and I feel myself close to release.

"That's enough now," I say in a rough voice, regretfully letting go of her two firm *sohuru*, hanging low over my face, the nipples close enough to take with my mouth (I don't, *bashtooh*, all deities help me, I don't)....

But she gasps for air and, between ragged breaths, continues squirming, pressing her own body over mine, moving unconsciously (or intentionally, *rawah bashtooh*, I don't know) . . . and then, to make matters worse, she puts her hand on my *varqooi* that's ready to burst.

As soon as she cups my accursed Imperial snake, I'm done for.

"No . . ." I suck in my breath sharply. "Don't do that. . . . No, don't. . . ."

But it's too late. I stiffen and explode . . . in my uniform pants.

Now that I have my mind back, my head and neck burn with embarrassment. I pull away, cover myself below, cover the *shebet* mess. "No, damn it, this *cannot* be happening!" I exclaim, then start to laugh bitterly at my own *shar-ta-haak* weakness.

What have I done?

No Kassiopei man may waste the so-called divine *phietei*, the seed of our bloodline. There are no such restrictions on other men in the general population, only us. We're instructed by the priests of Hel-Ra that we must use the sex act primarily to procreate under controlled circumstances. Outside the Rite of Sacrifice, the giving of our precious genetic material must be confined to a carefully chosen marriage partner. Any acts of erotic self-pleasuring must be minimal (being realistic—at times the Kassiopei *need* can be too great, so it happens) or avoided altogether. Right now, I've disgraced myself and committed a minor sacrilege to the cult of Kassiopei.

I've also shamed myself before Gwen Lark.

Like a fool, I tell her to get out—but first, to please cover herself and put the damn bra back on—while I turn away from her and lie on my side to face the wall. She fumbles with her clothing then goes to sit on my chair, resting her head against the desk, breathing quietly, as we wait out the few daydreams necessary for the initial effects of the Jump to lessen.

I continue to laugh silently, with my face against the wall, laugh and laugh, shaking with anger and humiliation.

"I'm sorry . . ." she says with emotion. "I am so sorry!"

"Not your fault," I mutter, flaming with self-anger. "It's all mine."

The wait period is finally over.

We know that both of us are absolutely embarrassed, humiliated. It's impossible to tell which one of us is worse off.

"You may go now," I tell her without looking in her direction.

Her voice sounds awkward, "Are you—are you okay?"

"It's only Jump sickness, Lark," I reply in a hard voice.

There is no way I am going to admit to weakness, not now, not ever.

"That was Jump sickness?" she asks, and though I don't see her face, I discern a tone of surprise.

Lie to her.

"Yes . . ." I say after the slightest pause. "Now, go! I am going to get *cleaned up* now, and you—you are going to *go*."

"Okay," she whispers.

And she flees my quarters.

This is the incident that makes it clear to me that she is my weakness, and I can do nothing about it.

THINGS ONLY GET MORE intense from there on. I harden myself against her, becoming cold as ice in her presence, because I must. And she—it appears, she takes it as a challenge to break me, crack my reserve, get past my walls.

She torments me.

The events speed up, and even our voice training time together, and the daily time spent at the CCO, develop our relationship into an inevitable direction.

The Red Quadrant Zero Gravity Dance brings everything into terrible focus, not only for me but for my closest friends. That's when I find out for a fact (thanks to Anu Vei's typically rude and timely commentary which I treasure) that Logan Sangre is now out of the picture. Apparently, Sangre and Lark broke up (*chuvuat*, Anu, my favorite *chazuf*), and that's when I also learn that Xelio asked Gwen Lark to be his date for the Dance. Either Xel wants to torment me a little in his usual loving way, or because he's genuinely interested in her.

If he is, what am I to do? I have my Imperial duty, while he is a free man, free to date or love anyone he likes (which he does, in his suave, practiced way which apparently so many women find irresistible).

And so is she.

On the day of the Dance, I try to avoid it altogether, but then steel myself and attend, because I must show up, being the Command Pilot of this vessel.

I arrive, with Ker and Oalla, all of us formally attired. Erita is not with us, having volunteered for supervisor duty of the skeleton crew on shift—which, according to Oalla, means she's moping, having "tragically" broken up with that Arbiter back in Poseidon, over interstellar comms. I half-envy Eri right now....

We make our way through the dancing crowds in the Resonance Chamber illuminated by every shade of red imaginable (until it hurts the eyes, to be honest), so that we could be inside the burning heart of a red dwarf star.

We see Xel getting a drink at one of the stations and stop to chat. This is Xel's busy night; as the senior Red Quadrant officer on this ship, he's in charge of the event. Fortunately, I don't see Lark anywhere at the moment, and it's for the best.

"So, Xel, where's your date?" Oalla asks suddenly. "Hope you didn't frighten her too badly with your delightful charming personality?"

Xel raises one brow, and then takes a step toward a female in a sleek dark red dress, standing with her back turned.

"There she is!" he says with a softening smile.

The girl turns around, to face us.

It's Gwen.

No, rawah bashtooh, *it can't be. She is a goddess.*

Gwen Lark is wearing exquisite High Court makeup, has her brown hair up in an intricate contraption worthy of an Imperial Assembly, and her dress—so dark red that it could be black—is showing off her perfect, soft skin.

Everyone is looking at her, but I'm only vaguely aware of them with my peripheral vision, because I am entirely focused on *her.*

She is *transformed.*

She is beautiful . . . So beautiful that it hurts. . . .

Why has it never occurred to me, after months of knowing her, that Gwen Lark is truly magnificent, exquisite beyond reason?

At my initial sight of her, I feel something strike me in the gut. So much so that I frown, grow perfectly still, and my mouth falls open.

I stare at her in disbelief, taking in her unearthly, painful beauty that *cuts into me* . . . and she looks back at me, with her amazing blue eyes. They are full of clarity, as always, but tonight they're also fearless and daring in their proud, taunting expression.

I dare you not to see me, her eyes communicate.

I honestly don't know what to do, what to say right now.

"Lark?" I finally ask. This is the stupidest question possible, and it reveals my confused, impacted state.

"Yes?" she says a little breathlessly, looking up at me. She is possibly flushed (or it could be all that red illumination) and a tiny little smile of triumph is dancing around her sweet, pouting, blood-red, gloss-covered lips.

Ah, those lips!

"I—I didn't recognize you, sorry," I say, as coldly as I can—at a time when in truth I'm molten, I've become the red star, and my flames have roared to life. And I continue staring at her with wide, dumbstruck, idiot eyes.

"Gwen Lark?" Oalla exclaims next to me. "Is that you? *No!* But, you look amazing! I didn't recognize you either, wow! What a gorgeous dress! And I love your makeup! You could be at the Imperial Court, looking like that!"

"Thank you," Gwen says softly, and her earrings glitter in her delicate earlobes, while a large red jewel slides deeper in the crevice between her *sohuru*. Helplessly, I visualize the time

I've seen them exposed, held those plump *sohuru* with my hands. . . . Right now, she is *vuchusei*, and I want to eat her up like a ripe fruit.

Next to me, Ker notices her transformation and checks out Lark appreciatively, and Oalla is also examining her closely. Good thing I know that Ker and Oalla are completely into each other, else I might have another reason for worry. . . .

"Here you go." Xelio interrupts the moment by handing Gwen her drink. Sly *chazuf* has gotten himself the perfect date, and the worst part is, right now he absolutely knows it.

Varqood. . . .

"Thanks," she says, glancing at him with a tantalizing, teasing smile (I am destroyed, seeing it). And then she adds, "Hey, do you know what time it is? My vocal performance is at 8:15."

She momentarily glances back at the rest of us, and we're all still staring at her.

Furthermore, *I* am staring at her.

I'm so still, so perfectly unbelievably *motionless*, that I think she notices. *What's wrong with me?*

"Don't worry," Xel tells her, checking his micro-scheduler that he pulls out of his pocket. "The performances begin at 8:00 PM, which is in ten minutes from now, and looks like you are the second person in the lineup."

"Great!" Lark smiles brightly, radiantly (so much so that it burns me, *bashtooh*) and she turns to all of us. "All right, you must hear me sing!"

"I wouldn't miss it for the world," Oalla says, smiling back at her. I can tell Keigeri is impressed with Lark tonight. And then Oalla sees me, still frozen motionless, still *looking at Lark*, and she nudges me on the arm. "Kass? Hey!"

"Yes?" I blink, stupidly tearing myself away from the glory

that is Gwen Lark and give my attention to my heart sister. It's almost a relief, not having to stare at the *sun*.

"We're going to stick around long enough to hear Lark perform, all right?" Oalla says, giving me an observant, meaningful look. Okay, why is it meaningful? What does she think right now? *Bashtooh*, has she recognized the extent of my besotted disaster?

I nod, stiffly. "That's fine." From now onward, I make a point of no longer looking at Lark at all.

We go to get drinks, and then I walk around the grand perimeter of the Resonance Chamber, in my official Command Pilot role, observing the crowds in the room.

I will not dwell on what she's doing right now, I will not.

Soon it will be time for her accursed song.

I TRY NOT TO LOOK, but I see her, and only *her*, despite myself.

Gravity is turned up to normal, so Gwen Lark dances with Vekahat on the dance floor. She is confident and energetic, and she seems to command their dance. Remarkable transformation, continued!

I glance constantly and see them moving together. Xel spins her skillfully (*varqood* him), while she dips and turns, and her diaphanous skirt flies like clouds of crimson summer pollen on the wind.

Sometimes it seems, during the turns, she glances around quickly, as if to see if someone is there.

She must sense my gaze upon her . . . She feels me looking.

I stand far off at the edge of the walkway, turned in her direction, making a hopeless effort to observe the entirety of the dancing crowd and not solely *her*.

But no, it's no use; I am looking directly at her.

Does she know?

She's felt the impact of my unmistakable Imperial Kassiopei gaze before. When I train its full force on someone, they *don't* forget. Even from this distance, she can probably see my unblinking eyes fixed relentlessly upon her, *watching*, piercing her.

And . . . it's as if she knows that I see her differently tonight, differently, at last. All those other times, I've seen Lark, my intimate, clear-eyed obsession. But now—now she is *divine*.

And yet, there is *no worship* in the intensity of my gaze.

Instead, there is strange, intimate *knowledge*.

I've taken her apart a million times and put her back together. I know the true Gwen underneath the radiant goddess, and she is even better.

I look at her now and she opens up to me like a blooming flower, across the distance, even if it's only in my mind.

And then, at last, she sings her song.

THE MOMENT IS HERE. It's Lark's turn to sing. She flirts with Xel briefly, then goes up the dais and steps onto the stage. She walks to the middle of the performer circle. Her heels make clicking noises that echo around the grand acoustics of the spherical chamber.

From my intentionally distant vantage point across the room, I watch her as she stands in the spotlight, glancing around at the huge crowd of teens, bathed in red glow. All attention is upon her.

She may or may not be terrified. She's certainly not showing it.

Just for a moment it seems that her gaze searches eagerly for a glimpse of someone in the crowd.

And—there I am. Our gazes touch for a fraction of an instant. Do I dare assume she recognizes me, or is it just my fevered imagination?

I'm "hiding out" on the distant walkway perimeter, next to Oalla Keigeri. Even if Lark were looking for me specifically, she would barely see me, standing so far in the distance, with my arms folded, my inner turmoil disguised with a casual stance.

I, on the other hand, will see her up-close, in just moments, thanks to the giant stadium screens.

Indeed—now everyone will see her and her splendor.

A weird stab of pointless, groundless possessiveness rips through me at the thought: *Everyone will see her. . . .*

She takes a deep breath, smiles, and taps her microphone pin on her dress.

Immediately, her face in all its dramatic, fiercely painted glory fills the giant screens along the perimeter. And the first rhythmic power-notes of an ancient Earth opera song called *Habanera* fill the chamber.

Gwen Lark begins to sing.

As I learn later, the *Habanera*, or *"L'amour est un oiseau rebelle,"* is an aria from a very popular Gebi opera *Carmen*, a song of seduction and freedom, a strange thing of paradox. "Love is a bird in rebellion," sings Carmen, the seductress—sultry, powerful, playful—while she's teasing and provoking a soldier who pretends to ignore her while he secretly desires her.

All ancient deities help me. . . .

Her rich mezzo soprano voice begins deep and low, rising from the depths of her chest. And then it pours forth like sweet *lvikao. . . .*

The song is a duel of power. Love, or the bird, comes and goes however it pleases. You set it free and it may or may not come back. You chase it, and it never does. But the moment you stop your pursuit, it pursues you.

This infernal song, truly, it can be a metaphor of our complex relationship.

During the first stanza, Lark stands motionless, finding her sound, it seems, controlling the perfect output of her voice. And then she loosens up and begins to stalk the stage, allowing her voice to take full control of *her*.

She becomes *fire*.

And I begin moving toward her—barely caring, only peripherally aware whether or not Oalla and Keruvat follow me.

Her voice soars, and the recorded orchestral accompaniment frames its rich timbre, while she turns in all directions and expresses the passion of Carmen.

No—it is her *own* passion, I'm certain of it, as I continue to make my way through the rapt audience, closer to the stage, closer to her. I need to be close to her.

I need. . . .

She is passion, she is Gwen, and Carmen is swallowed up and eclipsed.

Mindlessly, I'm drawn to her fiery glory, my body no longer mine as I push forward, until I'm at the foot of the stage.

As she moves fiercely about the stage, she glances down into the audience, to see the ocean of attentive faces, as both Gebi and Atlanteans watch her in fascination.

And then she sees *me*.

I stand directly before her, in the front row. The *daimon* are nearby too, but I am only half-aware, watching her with rapt attention.

What must she think?

Her daring gaze flashes in my direction once more.

I blink, and my lips part. . . . I am gazing at her in wonder.

It matters no longer if she sees my raw, vulnerable *need*. . . . In this moment, all my secret interior, my innermost layers are exposed. Through my infinitely focused gaze my long-submerged mystery finally comes to light.

She smiles and teases and seduces . . . and even when she turns away, I *know* she still sings to *me*.

With every new glance in my direction, more and more of my layers fall away before her.

I tremble, feeling the heat in my head and neck . . . and the corresponding flush and throbbing in my privates. *No, stop!* I must keep myself together or I will dissolve entirely before her. In those diffuse moments, as my last embers of control and reason slip away, I slam my will down over my own body. . . . I count in my mind, control my breath as I was taught by the Hel-Ra priests. But the sheer confusion of the moment and the resistance of my own body puts me under such strain that I feel ill. . . .

With all my being, I strive toward her, even as I fight myself. *To the death*. . . .

And then the music escalates, the music is on fire. . . . Gwen Lark sings fiercely, and her voice strikes the air like a whip, then modulates and purrs in the low register, alternating the moments of passion. She glances in my direction again. . . .

Accursed, beautiful *maatibri*.

Seductress.

My downfall.

I continue to look at her, transfixed. And then, because I've stopped trying to disguise that which is hopeless, my will having capitulated, I reveal the soul-deep, *bone*-deep uninhibited animal instinct level underneath all . . . and bring it forth at last.

My undisguised, dark *desire*.

And directly beneath all that (because there's no end to these levels, these *dimensions* of being), there is *something more*.

The truth.

I want her, desperately.

And she must know it now, with no more disguises left between us.

Maybe this awareness fuels her, because suddenly she seems even stronger; fierce, free, in wild rebellion against the former limits of her own self.

Her disguise has fallen away also.

The glorious, dark-haired young woman with the cherry-blood-and-crimson mouth blazing on the screens around the room, stretching her arms and throwing her head back while the grand sound pours from her, to fill every crevice of every object and every person in this chamber—she is *Gwen Lark*.

She always has been.

All this time she was hiding, but she is out, at last.

Lark ends her song on a triumphant high note that blasts away the last shadow of doubt, and the orchestra concludes the framing sound.

The crowd screams wildly, even before the music is over.

My body and soul are no longer mine.

No longer mine. . . .

And then, out of nowhere (possibly as a last defense against my own downfall) a terrible dawning of insight comes to me.

Her voice—it was a *maatibri* voice! All this time, these insane moments of her song, oozing with sensuality, and its unbelievable physical effect on me—she used the *desire* voice!

Fury strikes me, like a bucket of ice water. And just like that, my arousal is vanquished (not gone but subjugated sufficiently to make me again functional), because I know the true reason for it. It isn't *she*, or *my* own weakness, it's the *voice*, the accursed Logos voice, used cluelessly and irresponsibly to amplify a voice of *desire*. She's probably aroused the entire venue crowd with her inappropriate actions!

Suddenly, I must get away from her before I do something so disciplinary in my anger that I will regret it. Later—I will reprimand her about this later.

My last glimpse of Lark is of her impulsively grabbing the carnation flower that's tucked in her hair, before I turn my back on her. I never get to see her toss the flower out into the crowd (as I'm told later). Instead, exerting a merciless force—the last of my willpower, now aided by my anger—I head for the exit.

I walk through the crowd, followed by Oalla and Keruvat.

UNFORTUNATELY, I don't get away fast enough. Neither Ker nor Oalla must see my darkened mood, and so I permit myself to linger long enough for us to stop near the perimeter stations where Ker gets a drink refill in his tall covered glass.

"At this consumption rate, Ker-face, you're going to need to pee," Oalla says playfully, nudging him, then letting her hand slide fondly over the muscle of his upper arm.

"Since it's not my Quadrant . . . and I'm not on duty," Ker mumbles in between slurps through the straw, "frequent peeing is permitted. Nay, encouraged. You should try it."

Oalla snorts.

"Drink, Kass?" Ker wiggles one brow in my direction.

"I think I'll pass," I say with a calm flicker of amusement.

Ker slurps again. "You won't *pass* if you don't drink—"

Oalla rolls her eyes and pushes Ker toward the crowded

drink station. "Fine, get me a refill too. I'll just wait over there with the CP."

Oalla and I start moving toward a less crowded spot along the walkway, making casual comments about which I have no memory at all.

In that moment I see Xelio and Gwen coming in our direction. Immediately I feel a stab of emotion. Only, this time it's icy, and I'm fully in control.

Xel throws us a daring grin and winks at Gwen. "Wait here, *im nefira*, while I get your drink!" he intones loudly while nodding to the rest of us, as we stand off to the side. And off he goes into the crowd at the drink stations.

Oalla is telling me something about unfortunate Gebi choices of formal dress style and fabrics, just as Lark stops before us. Her breathing is still elevated and her eyes sparkle with excitement.

Im nefira indeed. . . . Even though I'm fuming with anger, her beauty still manages to take my breath away again, if only for a moment.

Oalla glances at Lark and one of her brows goes up, but she is smiling. "Wow!" she says to her. "Just, wow!"

She's obviously referring to Lark's performance. Why is Keigeri not more critical just now, after that *desire* voice display?

Just then, Gwen turns her lovely face and possibly notices my grave demeanor.

Yes, my face is averted slightly, arms folded at my chest, while I try to keep my gaze from making direct contact with hers and look off to the side.

After several heartbeats I decide to face her.

Frowning, I turn to her suddenly. And I allow her to see my *cold* expression, my barely leashed anger.

I feel implacable and dark, and I must look demonic as I stand before her.

She appears stunned. The sweet, pouting mouth falls slack, while all her joyous confidence and euphoria evaporate in the blink of an eye.

"*Lark.* We need to talk immediately. *Come!*" I say in a killing voice, making the decision to have the reprimand conversation here and now. I motion her to follow me as I start walking.

"Okay. . . ." she breathes, glancing briefly at Oalla, and follows me as we move off a few steps away.

Here I stop and turn to her.

"What you did out there—that was extremely *inappropriate*," I say, controlling myself enough to come across as reasonable, but my hard tone does not disguise my derision. "You used the *desire power voice* in public."

Her lips part. "I did what?"

How innocent and clueless she seems. Though, she might have done it without thinking or even being aware of her action, so I must continue being diplomatic, and give her the benefit of the doubt.

"The *desire voice* is only to be used in private, and only with individuals with whom you have an intimate relationship," I say, choosing careful, neutral words, while my gaze is boring down at her. "Do you understand what you've done? You've just shamed the crew, all these people, my entire ship—"

From behind, I hear Oalla's voice.

"Wait, Kass—what are you talking about?" Keigeri interrupts me suddenly. She obviously followed us, and is now looking from Lark to me with a slight frown. "But—she didn't!"

I freeze. A cold flood washes over me in that moment, as another realization strikes. I'm very quiet as I turn to look at the *daimon.* "What?"

"I mean, she *didn't* use a power voice," Oalla repeats, craning her neck at me and revealing a curiously perceptive expression. "Admittedly, it was a very lovely and strong voice, and Gwen sang that classical piece beautifully, but it was just a normal, unenhanced singing voice."

. . . a normal, unenhanced singing voice.

The words ring in my mind.

"But—" I say, pausing.

And suddenly I feel my face, my cheeks, my neck—all of me —filling with wild, ugly heat. My head is burning, which means I am flushed bright red, and it's probably noticeable even despite the brilliant red illumination in the room.

"I—" I attempt to speak, and it comes out in a strange, quiet voice, as I shake my head. "I—I must go, excuse me. . . ."

My mind is in disarray as the "logical" pieces spin and fall together and then fall apart.

For the last few daydreams, I had convinced myself with rational certainty that *desire* was not real, that *desire* was a manufactured artificial effect. And hence, I had nothing to worry about, I was off the hook for the wilderness of feelings in which I have been wandering, lost.

But no.

Desire was all *me*.

Still is.

I must get the *bashtooh* out of here at once. . . . Better yet, I must lock myself in my officers' quarters and never come out again, and never face Oalla or any of my *sen-i-senet*, or any of my subordinates, or . . . I must never face *her*.

Gwen Lark.

My obsession, my real undeniable weakness, my blazing desire.

And so, without looking at Lark or Oalla, I turn around like an inanimate, mechanical thing forged of shame and humiliation. I swiftly walk past them, and continue toward the exit doors of the Resonance Chamber.

In my mind, I'm not merely walking—I run.

As soon as I escape outside the noisy red inferno that is the Resonance Chamber, I make my way through the Command Deck to my own personal quarters.

Once in my cabin, I lock the door, and drop down powerlessly to sit on my chair. My temples race with an elevated pulse, the result of anxious, furious confusion. Even as I try to catch my breath, listening to the quiet hum of the air vents, soon enough my gaze falls on my narrow cot. At once, it evokes a flood of memories of what happened here between us many days ago, during the Jump.

Even here in my own cabin there is no relief for me. No escape from thoughts of *her*.

Everything reminds me of her. Of something about her. Minor soft details, sweet glimpses. . . .

I sit with my head lowered in my hands, pressing my temples angrily. Oh, if only I could pull all the knowledge, all my awareness of her out of my *garooi* head.

About half an hour later, there's a knock on my door.

I look up from my fevered daze, groaning silently, and say, "Come in."

Then I recall stupidly that the officers' cabin doors seal automatically with a secure auto-lock once someone is inside, so I get up and open the door.

It's Oalla Keigeri.

"Hey, Kass," she says quietly and carefully. "Sorry to barge

in but—are you okay?"

"Huh?" I say, frowning in confusion. Then I rub the bridge of my nose and nod at her. "Come in."

Oalla steps inside my quarters, and I relinquish my chair for her while I go sit on my cot.

"So," I say.

"So," she replies, crossing her legs. Her fabulous red outfit flows over her elegant knees.

There's a long moment of silence.

"Where's Ker?" I ask pointlessly.

"Back at the dance." Oalla shakes her head slightly and adjusts a few artful locks of her hair. "So," she repeats. "Why did you take off in such a hurry?"

"What do you mean?"

Keigeri gathers herself, and then trains the full force of her sisterly regard upon me. "What I mean is we need to talk about Gwen Lark."

"What?" My frown deepens. I lean forward on my low bed, my long legs bent at the knees because of my height, my hands together, fingers crossed, fingers tapping. . . .

But Oalla doesn't relent. "We need to talk about her. About you and her."

At once, I feel the rising flush of heat returning to drown my head.

"What's there to talk about?" I say roughly, looking down at Oalla's sparkling hemline, at her knees, her polished crimson nails. Anywhere but her perceptive eyes.

She sighs. "Okay . . . I'm worried about you. You were messed up for months, *years*, with Elikara. I don't want something like that to happen to you again, especially after what you went through at Ae-Leiterra. I know we don't talk about Ae-Leiterra—"

A stab of anger gives me the courage to look Keigeri in the eyes. "Elikara? What does Eli have to do with anything?" I say with soft outrage.

Oalla bites her lips, sighs again, cranes her neck to one side. "Kass . . . Command Pilot, with all due respect, you *know*. You have strong feelings—possibly to the same degree, maybe even more—the same, equally strong feelings for Gwen Lark as you had for Eli."

"I—" I start to contradict then trail off. My frown deepens. "This is *garooi*. There's nothing. Besides, Eli was a childhood thing. And this—"

"And this is not. Please," Oalla says gently. "It would really be better for everyone if you accepted—if you admitted how you feel."

"How I feel doesn't matter," I say in a hard voice. "Nothing *can* happen. And nothing will."

Oalla's expression is sympathetic. "I understand. But—keeping these kinds of feelings bottled up is not a solid long-term strategy, especially for your mental health. You and I both know that life is ridiculous. You already have to repress far too many things as part of your regular Imperial duties, *and* your Fleet duties. If you add a few more heavy weights to your burden—it might make your ridiculous life more *shar-ta-haak* than it already is. And, it will make all of us around you crazy with worry."

I listen to her in silence.

Oalla continues lecturing—nagging me—gently, "Feelings of affection must and will grow naturally up toward the light. If you force them to grow sideways, then they turn into *sha* that consume you and make you a real *chazuf*—not that you already aren't one." She laughs, trying to make me smile; I don't.

"So. There are *feelings*. Yes. What do you expect me to do?" I say wearily, looking at her with narrowed eyes.

"Not much." Oalla taps her fingers on her arm, pats down the split hem of her dress. "But—you might start by being kind to her—to Lark. The girl is a genuinely good human being, entirely harmless. She tries so hard—to be, to *do* things right, in every sense, and for everyone. And—from what I can tell, she has feelings for you too, no matter how underdeveloped or immature. She definitely thinks very highly of you."

"Don't say that. . . ." I shake my head. "The last thing I need to hear about is her feelings for me."

Keigeri smiles at me suddenly, a saucy, teasing smile. "Are you sure? I know you care what she thinks about you, how she *feels*."

"Enough," I say half-heartedly. I exhale, wipe my forehead with my splayed fingers. "Seriously, this is a *shebet* conversation."

Oalla leans forward and pats me on the knee. "I want you to be okay, Kass. I really, truly, awfully worry about you these days. Even Ker is noticing your *state*, and we all know Ker can be a dolt when it comes to these kinds of feelings. And Xel is taking advantage of you shamelessly. I told that boy not to ask Lark out as his date, but he told me to go mind my own business, and that she's free and unattached, and unless you make a move on her, he will."

"He said what?" I lean forward.

Oalla makes a sound of amusement. "No, he didn't say anything like that, of course, don't worry—I'm just a good mind reader. But you know how our little Xel has a way with the girls, so he just couldn't let a good one pass by without trying. And, from what I can tell, Xel might be a little in over his head here, with Lark. She is the real deal, and not one for playing games."

"Xel doesn't play games," I say. "Not anymore."

Oalla nods. "I know. But Xel can *sense* how you feel about her, and I think he wants to provoke you, just a tiny little bit. For old times' sake. The boy loves you, but he will always want to compete for everything. It's just how the two of you are made. Little boy-birds showing male feather displays to each other, ruffling each other's plumage."

"No, we're not—come *on*, Keigeri."

She chuckles. "All right, good to have you smiling even a little. Now that we have this out in the open, I want you to promise me, be kind to Gwen, treat her gently, let yourself *feel* something again. And—just see where it goes."

"It's not going anywhere," I say, and my faint smile fades. "You know it can never go anywhere because of who I am."

"Yes, my Imperial Lord and Command Pilot." Oalla says, with a tone that suggests she's humoring me, then stands up. "But sometimes there can be joy in the moment. And now, get some rest. When you see Gwen Lark tomorrow, give her a chance, and be yourself. Screw obligations, for once. *Nefero niktos*, Kass."

Before I can protest any further, Oalla heads for the door and shuts it after herself.

I remain alone with my thoughts and the quiet hum of the air vents. I try to do some basic work, check my console message feed.

It's getting late, so I prep for bed. As always, first I unroll the black armband around my sleeve, covering the tiny *astroctadra* pin inside, fold the black fabric and set it on my table. Then I remove my White Fleet uniform, the dress uniform used for special occasions—such as this Zero-G Dance.

I get in bed, wearing only shorts—since sleeping in the nude is impractical on a Fleet vessel. And then I lie there, restless, plagued by endless images and again, thoughts of the Gebi *maatibri*, Gwen Lark. Oalla's words reinforce so many things for me; the feelings—*my* feelings, I must own them—are indeed out in the open now, and too many people close to me are aware of them.

She's also right about Elikara, my first romantic affection. Except, my emotions for Eli were never expressed in such a physical way as this. Granted, I fantasized about kissing and holding Elikara many times during our school years; indeed, my body felt some budding urges. But not like this, never like this. . . .

What is Lark doing now? My racing thoughts rebound to her. Is she still with Xel, finishing up the wild evening?

I visualize the beauty of her, the impossible, *vuchusei* beauty of her face and form . . . her line of hips, her sweetly prominent *sohuru* with the deep red jewel plunged between them, glittering against her smooth skin.

And the more I try to stop thinking, the more my mind burns in a fever.

Xel called her *im nefira*. . . .

No, she's mine.

I begin to utter in my mind, *im nefira, im nefira, im nefira*. . . .

I imagine taking her by the slim arms (her skin is so soft), dancing with her in the grand expanse of red, as the gravity falls away and we soar up to the red dome ceiling. I pull her closer to me, and with dream logic everyone else in the chamber is no longer there. We're in a private world of sensuality, only the two of us. I press her body against mine, so she floats, a divine *maatibri*, her hair loose from its coiffure. . . .

Moments later, I put my hands on her and start ripping away the spider silk blood-red fabric of her clinging dress, at the same time as she rips away my formal White uniform, and we start touching flesh. . . .

I lie in my cot, my heart pounding, and instead of sleep I feel my *varqooi* stiffening.

Rawah bashtooh. . . .

I begin the relaxation technique exercises taught to me by the priests of Kassiopei. Think boring thoughts about inanimate objects. Do mathematics in your mind. Slowing down the breath eases the arousal. . . .

But not tonight.

I am furious at myself. Nothing is working.

I get out of bed, throwing off my blanket. And then I stand and breathe, in and out, deeply, then slowly, count each shuddering breath. I consider going in the wash stall and taking a cold shower.

I take the few steps, pause again. Instead, I stand over the sink and expose myself. As soon as my shorts are down, the swollen *varqooi* stands up rigid over my equally stiff *phietei*-sack. I take it roughly and get to work. Just a few strokes later, I finish hard . . . splattering the sink.

My mind rebounds briefly, but it's not enough. Accursed Kassiopei stamina—it causes my body to respond again in less than a daydream. I begin to stroke again, filled with self-fury, not giving a damn about the sacrilege of wasting the divine Imperial Kassiopei *phietei*, or the mess in the sink.

Eventually, I run the water and clean myself up.

This is the one and only time I have allowed myself this transgression against the cult of my Dynasty in the many months since the last Rite of Sacrifice.

All because of Gwen Lark, my out-of-control desire for her. . . .

I'm no longer in command of myself.

≈

MY MEMORIES of that time surge, and with them a surge of memory-lust washes over me. . . . Yes, even here in the present, only days away from our arrival on Atlantis. However, my Father's conversation and the resulting decision I have to make tonight is hanging over me, so my lustful memories are manageable.

And so I plunge back into the sweetly painful ocean of a different memory. . . .

After the events of the Red Zero-G Dance, it's hard to recall what the consequent days bring, because I have to maintain my cool with Lark in public.

And then the season changes, the Yellow Zero-G Dance takes place only a few short days ago, and even more things come to light.

I attend the dance in a bleak mood, with all that's in Atlantis hanging over me, all my grim duties to come.

Of course, Gwen Lark is there with her Earth friends, everyone wearing blinding gold. I manage to avoid her for most of the evening. However, in the golden yellow bubble of the Resonance Chamber, without needing to be prompted by meaningful looks from Oalla and Ker, I finally feel the inevitable pull and go toward her.

I am fully aware she watches me across the room as I approach.

In moments, I stand before her.

My expression is carefully veiled, but at the sight of her my breath catches with intensity—I drink in all of her. Tonight, she is a soft beauty—not a crimson-clad *maatibri* but gentle Amrevet, the youthfully eternal goddess, framed by the golden dress, glittering hair, understated makeup. I steel myself against her subtle, even more potent onslaught, but nevertheless a flush of heat washes over me.

Breathe, shar-ta-haak, *just breathe.*

"Lark . . ." I say, keeping my voice steady, composed.

"Command Pilot. . . ." Her voice is soft and unassuming.

I take a deep breath. Then, without warning, I sit down in the seat next to her.

There is a weird moment as her eyes widen, while she stares straight ahead of her.

My face is turned toward her. All my attention is fixed upon her face, as I watch her closely . . . and say nothing.

"I'm surprised you're still here at the Dance," she suddenly blurts out, not quite glancing at me. "I thought you hated these things."

"For the most part, yes, I prefer to leave as quickly as possible." I continue looking at her as I speak, so that now she must also turn to face me.

"I suppose you have to dance so much at Court," she mutters.

Oh, her sweet innocent expression, those perfect pink lips!

"Yes . . . too much," I reply.

There is an awkward pause. The world has narrowed in on us, and suddenly it *feels* too much.

"So," I say, looking slightly away and down, stupidly examining the floor so as not to meet her earnest, clear-eyed gaze. "How does it feel? A week remains. A week of *freedom,* and then we arrive in Atlantis."

"I don't know," she says. "Not sure what to think, actually. My fate, all of our fates as Earth refugees—they are the great unknown. At least you can return to your home and normal life."

A stab of irony and regret strikes me in the gut.

"Ah. My *normal* life. . . ." I look up again, not sure what she might see in my eyes, what kind of vulnerability. "My normal life indeed awaits."

"I understand." She nods. "You must have so many unimaginable duties, so much additional responsibility . . . being who you are."

"And who am I?" I ask, stifling a surge of bitterness, as my eyes bore into hers, my gaze overwhelming her with its force, so that she blinks.

"You are—the Imperial Crown Prince," she says.

"Yes," I say, speaking plain facts. "It is who I *am*. I may play at everything else—soldier, commander, pilot. But the one thing that I cannot escape is the fate of Imperial Kassiopei."

And I grow silent, my mouth curved in a bitter smirk. I have never been so strangely frank with her, as I am in these bizarre moments.

"Gravity changing now!"

The playful disembodied voice of the Music Mage comes from the air around us. And immediately the beat of the music slows down while a physical sense of falling intrudes on our strange conversation.

The strands of my loose hair begin to float lightly around my back and shoulders as I make the slightest movements. . . .

Her own dark tendrils, sweet and rich like well-brewed *lawu*, also rise about her shoulders as she turns her head, swept up by the low gravity.

"But there must be so many wonderful aspects about being who you are," she says softly after that small pause. "So much good that you can do for all your people with the power at your disposal. . . ."

"Oh, yes. Always so optimistic, Lark." I look at her sideways with a broken, fake smile. "First and foremost, I can do what all Kassiopei do, and that is, perpetuate the bloodline. All that precious Imperial genetic material must not go to waste."

She frowns slightly, tensing up. It must be a real effort to maintain our impossible talk. "Is it true," she asks suddenly, "that you have to get married soon?"

Ah, and there it is. . . .

I blink, look down at my hands, flex my fingers. "Yes." And then I turn to her again, watching her sideways, while individual strands of my long, *shar-ta-haak* Kassiopei hair float everywhere around me, getting in my face. "I will announce my beautiful Bride as soon as we arrive in Atlantis. What do you think about that, Lark?"

"I—" Her breath stumbles, while she appears to be struggling, gripped with some complex emotion. "I wish you all happiness and all the best. Congratulations. . . . You must love each other very much. . . ."

"Oh, yes," I reply, with barely concealed agony in my eyes. "Lady Tirinea Fuorai and I . . . we are—" My words trail away.

"I think I saw you speaking to her once," she interjects softly, awkwardly. "She seems very beautiful, amazing."

I smile because I must, a faint ghost smile. "Oh, she *is*." I utter each word with a measured, barely-leashed force, all the while looking at Lark with a merciless gaze. "And I can't wait to see her, as soon as we get back. . . . Even now, I want to hold her with my hands . . . feel her mouth against my teeth, and press her against the wall—"

I'm not speaking of Tirinea Fuorai, of course. The images in my mind betray me. I weaponize and use my sensual vision of Lark against herself.

And as I say these words, knowing they are painful, they will wound her, I'm glad, because I want them to hurt.

I want her to stop *feeling*. . . . That is, if she even feels anything for me, I want her to *stop*.

This, all of this must stop.

She appears stricken. Indeed, she seems ready to cry. . . .

And yet, she continues to look at me, because—I don't know why she still looks at me. There appears to be a sea change in her, something inevitable taking place inside her. . . .

And because it hurts, and I can feel how much it hurts *her* (hence, it hurts me), I stop.

"No," I say suddenly, and my voice goes dark as this time I visualize Lady Tirinea Fuorai with all her terrible beauty and artifice. "I *don't* want any of it. I *don't* want *her*—not with all her beauty and riches and genetic nobility and empty false smiles. But—I *must*. I must take her as my Consort, my Bride, and eventually my Wife, and I must *breed* her relentlessly until she produces fat litters of healthy children with perfect DNA for my Father to take comfort and pride in, to know that the divine Kassiopei bloodline continues well into the next generation. . . ."

I cut off the avalanche of words, and stand up suddenly. My hair billows around me in an angry golden cloud that I cannot escape.

I stand before her, open to her, holding nothing back in my eyes.

She watches me with parted lips, appearing stunned by what I just said, even dizzy from seeing my face swim above hers. . . .

"Gravity changing now. . . ."

This time, the words of the Music Mage slither through the air as the music slows down completely, and the low gravity starts fading into perfect weightlessness.

"Enough bitter nonsense spoken for tonight," I say, looking

down at her with a complex mixture of pain and fierce intensity. "My apologies for spoiling your mood, Lark. Have a good night."

And then I turn my back on her and start to walk away.

No!

Suddenly, I stop. A new madness has come over me, and it drives me to act in a way I've never permitted myself before.

I turn around.

And like the force of the tide, inevitable, I come back, looking at Gwen Lark with the enormity of a universe contained in my eyes.

"Oh, what's the use . . ." I mutter softly, addressing *myself* out loud like a *hoohvak*, making a helpless gesture with my hand.

I stop again before her, and this time reach out with my hand, palm up. "Come, Lark," I say. "Dance with me—for the *first* and *last* time."

She glances down at my outstretched hand in *wonder*, and then she looks up into my eyes.

She stands up, while the winds seem to gather and stir around her, and the haunting song that plays from the walls of the spherical chamber is "Caribbean Blue" by Gebi artist Enya.

And she takes my hand—at which point I feel a shock, and so does *she*, I'm certain—as for the first time, the warm, hard grasp of my larger fingers closes around her slender, vulnerable ones, as I lead her onto the dance floor and into the aerial realm of awe. . . .

I HOLD her by the hand—a gentle tug is all that's required to launch us upwards over the honey lake of light below, while the floor sinks deeper down and falls away completely.

And then I pull her closer, and my other hand comes

around her fragile waist ... and the mere touch sends shocks of electricity through all of me. I'm flushed with warmth, as if a sun liquified and spilled inside me, filling me with roaring light.

My hands ... touching her ... I am touching her.

We start circling gently to the ethereal rhythm of the waltz, and I pull her in closer and closer with each turn, so that now my pale hair is mingling with her glorious dark locks, and her face is inches away from mine, as I stare directly into her eyes. We are enclosed in a cocoon of floating strands and melody, and I feel her gentle breath wash softly over my lips until I tremble with fierce agony that I understand very well. ...

She is *nothing* and *everything*, a precious thing of air and breath, and all I have to do is pull her in closer yet, to close the distance of just another microscopic space between us that's separating us, and she will *dissolve* into me. ... While it still exists, that tiny distance between us is the equivalent of infinity.

Her hand that's held tightly in mine feels like it's now *on fire*, and I experience a corresponding, overwhelming flood of sensation and warmth coursing between us. Her other hand, gentle and so tentative in its ethereal touch, rests on my shoulder shyly, her trembling fingers tangled in my hair. ...

Oh, pull me in, my thoughts race in a fever, even as we soar toward the ceiling, where the honey flow of light has turned to rich, deep amber—ripe, sweet light.

Closer, closer, please. ...

I watch her face, mesmerized. She has opened up to me with a gentle *intimate* expression that's intended only for *me*, and her eyes, her forthright and clear blue eyes that I've seen so many years ago in my dying fever dream at Ae-Leiterra and recognized only later ... her eyes, they are—

Im amrevu.

"Lark ..." I whisper, my breath washing against her lips, just as we rise close enough to touch the ceiling with its orbs of champagne bubbles and vines of cascading grapes.

And still holding her waist tightly, I let go of her hand . . . because I must.

I must do this. . . . Or I will die again, a thousand deaths at Ae-Leiterra.

Just once.

I brush my fingertips against the side of her cheek, making her tremble, while fever rises, and this time it is not my lower body that takes over, it's my heart.

An ache of longing starts deep inside my chest where my heart beats a drum rhythm of life.

Time fragments and all times mix as one, in a *pegasei* cloud of rainbow light.

I am at once a pale-haired boy with knowing eyes, a young man with a burning snake of lust, a cold elder Imperator full of agonizing duty and immeasurable distance, a silent savior with a black band worn only by the ancient dead. . . .

I am all of them and more, because as I look at her now, indomitable like a mountain and yet so *lost*—I look *inside* her, and through her, and somehow I *know* her in that instant, more than she knows herself.

She is the awkward young woman with the bony elbows, skinny arms, and poor posture, the stooping shoulders and the anxiety-filled babble of words issuing out of her. She is the empathetic friend and the curious, inquisitive life-long student. She is the contradicting and stubborn warrior on behalf of her loved ones, a relentless force of truth, defying me at every turn, making me question my actions, my motives, my very *purpose*.

She is my force of change and anchor of what is real.

She is my everything.

"This cannot end," I whisper, following the trail of my

fingers with my breath, as I speak close into her ear, kind words like drops of rain, softly falling.

Her eyes . . . they are perfectly *loving* and perfectly clear.

In that moment at last she *knows* me also.

She breathes deeply and her lungs expand raggedly with each inhalation. She shudders as she sees the dying light in me, and I sense that she will weep in heartbeats from now. . . .

"Please . . ." she says. And it seems she doesn't even know what she's asking.

Please don't let go. . . .

In response, my hand tightens around her waist. Our mingling breath and the air between us, it is now my entire world.

"Lark . . ." I repeat again, and I am drowning. "I—"

"Gravity changing now!"

. . . I love you.

The words of the Music Mage cut me off, and it's just as well. That phrase—it cuts me off, and indicates the end.

The end of the song.

The end of the haunting music.

The end of us.

At once gravity starts to bloom, and with a shudder we both grasp each other's hands and begin the soft descent, at the same time as the floor starts rising up gently toward us.

All the meanwhile as we slow down our circling, she continues to stare into my eyes, with an innocent, intimate, desperate gaze.

At last, we stand on the dance floor. Breathing, breathing. . . .

I still hold one of her hands as I lead her back to the perimeter walkway.

Here I stop and look at her again.

"Thank you for the dance, Lark," I say in a numb voice.

"Thank you . . ." she echoes me softly. Her voice has lost all its resonance and is leached of energy. I feel her *loss* already, the fading of the touch and the growing distance.

But then I must ask one more thing, and it makes her pause and freeze in place.

"Whatever has happened between you and Sangre," I say, "I hope it did not hurt you deeply. I am very sorry about it. You deserve to be happy. Whatever has happened, it is none of my business—"

"*You* happened," she says suddenly, finding her voice. And her eyes are blazing, *wild*.

I grow still. An unbelievable wonder fills me.

It cannot be. . . .

"*You* happened between us," she repeats. "Logan and I broke up because of *you*."

My lips part. I blink.

Astonishment and *insight* and *hope* fill me.

Hope, hope, it blazes brighter than Helios fire!

My universe has opened a new dimension, like the vast river of being that the *pegasei* showed me.

However, I must keep it inside, for the moment. It is too precious, too fragile to risk.

And so, I only shake my head and nod to her. Without saying another word (brimming with glory and light) I turn away from *my* Lark and begin walking swiftly through the crowd.

She remains standing behind me, but I don't dare to look behind for fear of losing her fragile wonder.

∾

I SNAP BACK inside my mind, to the present moment here and now, in my cabin on board ICS-2, almost back to Atlantis.

Enough. No more memories.

I stare at the black piece of silken fabric that is my armband, my honor and integrity and my duty rolled into one simple square package.

The decision is at hand.

No more lying to myself.

I've chosen duty all my life, and I've never betrayed it. And now, I'm choosing duty again, as I always must.

Except—true duty lies with my conscience, soul, and heart. Not what my Father and the Imperial Dynasty dictates, but that which is *real.*

And my soul triumvirate guides me to fulfill my purpose, beyond time and beyond this one lifetime.

I choose you, Gwen Lark.

Im amrevu.

You are mine, and I am claiming you.

I am yours, as you have claimed me with one look of your clear, beloved eyes, so long ago.

And now . . . I must tread carefully in the next few days to make it happen, and I might even have to deceive and hurt you emotionally in the process to keep our fragile secret from my Father. But—only briefly, just for a bit; forgive me in advance, my love.

And thinking of the devious intricacy of what I must do, I smile.

The black armband lies folded before me, an anchor of memories, encompassing the burdened past. But already I am far beyond it, having stepped forth from the *black* and into the *light.*

The End of AESON: BLACK

Want to start from the beginning?
Catch up with your <u>free</u> copy of QUALIFY,
book one of The Atlantis Grail!

*More **TAG novellas** and **novels** coming soon,*
including the 5th full-length TAG novel!

*But first—a new **prequel series** exploring the events of Ancient*
Atlantis, 12,500 years ago, begins in:

EOS (Dawn of the Atlantis Grail, Book One)
Coming soon!

While you wait . . . for a change of pace, try the intensely romantic historical epic fantasy **Cobweb Bride** . . . or the madly hilarious **Vampires are from Venus, Werewolves are from Mars.**

$\sim$

Don't miss another book by Vera Nazarian!

Subscribe to the mailing list to be notified when the next books by Vera Nazarian are available.
We promise not to spam you or chit-chat, only make occasional book release announcements.

Want to talk about it with other fans?
Join the fun at . . .
The Atlantis Grail Fan Discussion Forum

GLOSSARY OF ATLANTEO WORDS

The following *Atlanteo* language words are used in this novella, listed in alphabetical order:

Archaeon Imperator – see *Imperator*.

Archaeona Imperatris – see *Imperatris*.

Astra daimon – an informal brotherhood and sisterhood of the best pilots in the Star Pilot Corps. You cannot join, you may only be chosen.

Astroctadra – a four-point star shape, in both two and three dimensions.

Atlantida – the Atlantean term for Atlantis, the planet, and for Imperial *Atlantida*, the nation.

Bakris – carrion

Bashtooh – common expletive, insult.

Chazuf – jerk, a-hole, generic crude term for guy, can be an insult or affectionate.

Chuvuat – thank you.

Dea – day

Eos – morning

Eos bread – breakfast

Eos pie – a kind of hand pie, usually fruit-filled.

Garooi – stupid

Gebi – earthling, something that came from Earth, in Classical *Atlanteo*.

Hoohvak – idiot, fool.

Im amrevu – my beloved.

Im nefira – my beauty.

Imperator – monarch sovereign ruler of Imperial *Atlantida*. Full title: *Archaeon Imperator*.

Imperatris – female monarch sovereign ruler of Imperial *Atlantida*, or consort spouse of the reigning *Imperator*. Full title: *Archaeona Imperatris*.

Kassiopeion – temple of the Kassiopei cult of divinity.

Kemetareon – the great square Imperial Kemet Forum, a part of an ultra-modern convention center-like complex of several stadiums, theaters, exhibit halls, and connecting buildings, located in downtown Poseidon.

Kefarai – freshman (plural, singular, collective, masculine, feminine) slang for First Year student such as Fleet Cadet.

Lawu – a deep brown ale.

Lvikao – an Atlantean caffeinated hot drink similar to both coffee and cocoa, with complex spices and the aroma of a pastry shop.

Maatibri – seductress

Mamai – mother

Nefero niktos – good evening, good night.

Pegasei – quantum trans-dimensional aliens introduced in the main series.

Phietei – male sperm, genetic material.

Rawah bashtooh – "very much" *bashtooh*, an amplified version of *bashtooh*.

Qvaali – mildly alcoholic beverage that is dark plum-colored, foams, smells like hops, wheat, and raspberries, and tastes like apple cider with a hint of berries and wheat. Aeson's favorite drink.

Scolariat – class

Sha – generic term for an animal that is a predator.

Shar-ta-haak – buffoon, fool, stupid, idiot.

Sen-i-senet – brothers and sisters.

Shebet – crap (a piece of), junk.

Shibet – a person made of crap (son of).

Sohuru – breasts

Stadion – stadium, also proper name of the biggest stadium in the Atlantis Grail complex, officially known as The Atlantis Grail Stadium.

Varqood – very strong expletive, an obscenity, the f-word.

Varqooi – crude term for male organ

Viatoios – orichalcum-based alloy, bullet-proof, blade-proof, and fire-proof silvery fabric material used for fine body armor and other protective gear.

Vuchusei – sweet, tasty, pleasurable, soulful, can be used as a sensual term in the erotic sense.

Wixameret – welcome

OTHER BOOKS BY VERA NAZARIAN

Lords of Rainbow

Dreams of the Compass Rose

Salt of the Air

The Perpetual Calendar of Inspiration

The Clock King and the Queen of the Hourglass

Mayhem at Grant-Williams High (YA)

The Duke in His Castle

After the Sundial

Mansfield Park and Mummies

Northanger Abbey and Angels and Dragons

Pride and Platypus: Mr. Darcy's Dreadful Secret

Vampires are from Venus, Werewolves are from Mars

A Comprehensive Guide to Attracting Supernatural Love

Cobweb Bride Trilogy:

Cobweb Bride

Cobweb Empire

Cobweb Forest

The Atlantis Grail:

Qualify (Book One)

Compete (Book Two)

Win (Book Three)

Survive (Book Four)

The Atlantis Grail Novella Series

Aeson: Blue

Aeson: Black

The Atlantis Grail Superfan Extras

The Atlantis Grail Companion

(Forthcoming)

Dawn of the Atlantis Grail (TAG Prequel Series)

Eos (Book One)

Dea (Book Two)

Niktos (Book Three)

Ghost (Book Four)

Starlight (Book Five)

The Atlantis Grail:

The Book of Everything (Book Five)

The Atlantis Grail Novella Series

Xelio: Red

Brie: Red

Thank you for your support!

ABOUT THE AUTHOR

Vera Nazarian is a two-time Nebula Award® Finalist, a Dragon Award 2018 Finalist, and a member of Science Fiction and Fantasy Writers of America. She immigrated to the USA from the former USSR as a kid, sold her first story at 17, and has been published in numerous anthologies and magazines, honorably mentioned in Year's Best volumes, and translated into eight languages.

Vera made her novelist debut with the critically acclaimed *Dreams of the Compass Rose* (2002), followed by *Lords of Rainbow* (2003). Her novella *The Clock King and the Queen of the Hourglass* made the 2005 Locus Recommended Reading List. Her debut collection *Salt of the Air* contains the 2007 Nebula Award-nominated "The Story of Love." Recent work includes the 2008 Nebula Finalist novella *The Duke in His Castle*, science fiction collection *After the Sundial* (2010), *The Perpetual Calendar of Inspiration* (2010), three Jane Austen parodies, *Mansfield Park and Mummies* (2009), *Northanger Abbey and Angels and Dragons* (2010), and *Pride and Platypus: Mr. Darcy's Dreadful Secret* (2012), all part of her *Supernatural Jane Austen Series*, a parody of self-help and supernatural relationships advice, *Vampires are from Venus, Werewolves are from Mars: A Comprehensive Guide to Attracting Supernatural Love* (2012), *Cobweb Bride Trilogy* (2013), the bestselling international cross-genre phenomenon series

The Atlantis Grail, now optioned for development as a feature film and/or TV series, *Qualify* (2014), *Compete* (2015), *Win* (2017), and *Survive* (2020), the novella *Aeson: Blue* (2021) and *The Atlantis Grail Companion* (2021).

After many years in Los Angeles, Vera now lives in a small town in Vermont. She uses her Armenian sense of humor and her Russian sense of suffering to bake conflicted pirozhki and make art.

In addition to being a writer, philosopher, and award-winning artist, she is also the publisher of Norilana Books.

Official website: https://www.veranazarian.com

Get on my Mailing List! https://www.veranazarian.com/signup.html

The Atlantis Grail Fan Discussion Forum:

https://atlantisgrail.proboards.com/

Astra Daimon and Shoelace Girls (Facebook fan group):

https://www.facebook.com/groups/adasg/

The Atlantis Grail – SPOILERS (Facebook fan group):

https://www.facebook.com/groups/tag2spoilers

TAG official website: https://www.theatlantisgrail.com/

TAG Fandom website: https://www.tag.fan

Norilana Books: https://www.norilana.com/

Twitter: https://twitter.com/Norilana

Facebook: https://www.facebook.com/VeraNazarian

TikTok: https://www.tiktok.com/@veranazarian

Instagram: https://www.instagram.com/vera_nazarian/

YouTube Channel: https://www.youtube.com/veranazarian-tag

Scan Code for Linktree.

ACKNOWLEDGMENTS

There are so many of you whose unwavering, loving support helped me bring this book to life. My gratitude is boundless, and I thank you with all my heart (and in alphabetical order, because in any other way lies madness)!

To my absolutely brilliant first readers, advisors, topic experts, editors, proofreaders, fandom moderators, and friends, Elizabeth Logotheti, Heather Dryer, Jeanne Miller, Nancy Huett, Nydia Fernandez Burdick, Roby James, Shelley Bruce, Susan Franzblau, Teri N. Sears, and West Yarbrough McDonough.

To my wonderful producer Richard Joel of 405 Productions who is working hard to make the film project a reality.

To all the amazing and hardworking ConCom volunteers of our annual TAG Con convention.

To the lovely and wonderful group of Vermont writers and friends, Anne Stuart, Ellen Jareckie, Lina Gimble, and Valerie Gillen, and to my dear friends in more distant places, Lisa Silverthorne and Patricia Duffy Novak.

To all the wonderful and enthusiastic members of the "Astra Daimon and Shoelace Girls" Facebook group, "The Atlantis Grail - SPOILERS" Facebook group, and the official TAG Discussion Forum on ProBoards.

To my awesome and fabulous Wattpad friends and fans who keep re-reading each TAG preview chapter and making me smile, laugh, and otherwise delight in your hilarious, stunning, amazing, and insightful responses to the story! Thank you immensely!

If I've forgotten or missed anyone, the fault is mine; please know that I love and appreciate you all.

Finally, I would like to thank all of you dear reader friends, who decided to take my hand and step into my world of The Atlantis Grail.

My deepest thanks to all for your support!
Before you go, you are kindly invited to leave a
review of this book!

Reviews are a wonderful way to help the author! They are also an exciting opportunity to share your honest thoughts with other readers, so **please post yours**, in as many places as possible, including TikTok and Instagram!